WICKED TEMPTATIONS

Task Force Hawaii Book 5

MELISSA SCHROEDER

Edited by
NOEL VARNER

Cover Art by
SCOTT CARPENTER

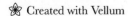

To the original Tamilya-
You were always the nicest girl and I never understood why you would hang with a degenerate like me. Now that we are all grown up, I am still a degenerate and you are still one of the nicest women I know. I have always been proud to call you my friend. I hope my Tamilya makes you happy.
Mel

Contents

Also by Melissa Schroeder

THE HARMLESS WORLD

The Original Harmless Five

- A Little Harmless Sex
- A Little Harmless Pleasure
- A Little Harmless Obsession
- A Little Harmless Lie
- A Little Harmless Addiction

Rough 'n Ready

- Rough Submission
- Rough Fascination
- Rough Fantasy
- Rough Ride

Harmless Trouble

- Harmless Secrets
- Harmless Revenge
- Harmless Scandals

The Wulf Family

- Faith
- Taboo
- Trust

A Little Harmless Military Romance

- Infatuation

- Possession
- Surrender

Task Force Hawaii

- Seductive Reasoning
- Hostile Desires
- Constant Craving
- Tangled Passions
- Wicked Temptations
- Twisted Emotions

TFH Team Bravo

- Justified Secrets-coming soon

THE CAMOS AND CUPCAKES WORLD

Camos and Cupcakes

- Delicious
- Luscious
- Scrumptious

The Fillmore Siblings

- Hate to Love You
- Love to Hate You

Juniper Springs

- Wild Love
- Crazy Love
- Last Love
- Imperfect Love

- Tempted

Mafia Sisters

- Stealing Destiny
- Guarding Fable

Faking It

- Faking it with my Billionaire Boss
- Faking it with my Brother's Best Friend
- Faking it with my Frenemy

The Fighting Sullivans

- Falling for the General's Daughter
- Falling for the Girl Next Door
- Falling for my Best Friend
- Falling for my Baby Mama

Also Included

- Kiss my Tinsel
- Dad Bod Rockstar

Texas Temptations

- Conquering India
- Delilah's Downfall

Hawaiian Holidays

- Mele Kalikimaka, Baby

- Sex on the Beach
- Getting Lei'd

Once Upon an Accident

- The Accidental Countess
- Lessons in Seduction
- The Spy Who Loved Her

The Cursed Clan

- Callum
- Angus
- Logan
- Fletcher
- Anice

The Sweet Shoppe

- Tempting Prudence
- Cowboy Up
- Her Wicked Warrior

By Blood

- Desire by Blood
- Seduction by Blood

Hands On

- The Hired Hand
- Hands on Training

Telepathic Cravings

- Voices Carry
- Lost in Emotion
- Hard Habit to Break

Bounty Hunters, Inc

- For Love or Honor
- Sinner's Delight

Saints and Sinners

- Seducing the Saint
- Hunting Mila

Lonestar Wolf Pack

- Primal Instincts

Texas Heat

- Scorched

Spies, Lies, and Alibis

- The Boss

Single Titles

- A Calculated Seduction
- Chasing Luck
- Going for Eight
- Grace Under Pressure
- Operation Love
- Saving Thea
- Snowbound Seduction
- Sweet Patience
- The Last Detail
- The Seduction of Widow McEwan

Hawaiian Terms

Aloha - Hello, goodbye, love
Bra-Bro
Bruddah- brother, term of endearment
Haole-Newcomer to the islands
Howzit - How is it going?
Kama'āina-Local to the islands
Mahalo-Thank you
Malasadas- A Portuguese donut without a hole which started out as a tradition for Shrove (Fat) Tuesday. They are deep fried, dipped in sugar or cinnamon and sugar. In other words, it is a decadent treat every person must try when they go to Hawaii. If you do not try it, you fail. Do yourself a favor. Go to Leonard's and buy one. You are welcome.
Pupule - crazy
Slippahs - slippers, AKA sandals

MEET THE TEAM

CAPTAIN
Martin "Del" Delano

Second in Command
Lt. Adam Lee

Regular Team Members
Graeme McGregor
Marcus Floyd
Cat Kalakau
Tamilya Lowe

Medical Team
Dr. Elle Middleton
Drew Franklin

Forensics
Charity Edwards

Contractors
Emma Taylor

Help with Hawaiian Terms

Aloha - Hello, goodbye, love
Bra-Bro
Bruddah- brother, term of endearment
Haole-Newcomer to the islands
Howzit - How is it going?
Kamaʻāina-Local to the islands
Mahalo-Thank you
Malasadas- A Portuguese donut without a hole which started out as a tradition for Shrove (Fat) Tuesday. They are deep fried, dipped in sugar or cinnamon and sugar. In other words, it is a decadent treat every person must try when they go to Hawaii. If you do not try it, you fail. Do yourself a favor. Go to Leonard's and buy one. You are welcome.
Pupule - crazy
Slippahs - slippers, AKA sandals

Acknowledgments

This book took longer than I wanted, but it would not have even happened without the help of so many people.

First, a big shout out to my editor Noel Varner for starting the book all over again when we both realized it wasn't what it should be. I would have never been able to finish it without you. Thanks to Scott Carpenter for my beautiful cover.

Thanks to Joy Harris and Brandy Walker for always supporting me and keeping me sane during some of the worst of times. And a big wet kiss to the Addicts for supporting me.

And of course, there is always Les who helped me through everything this last year and a half. I would not be here if it wasn't for you.

Acknowledgments

Prologue

"What do you mean I'm suspended?" Tamilya Lowe asked her supervisor Addie March.

"It's out of my hands and it is pissing me off," she muttered.

The last few days had worn heavily on Addie. In her late forties with a long career with the FBI under her belt, she always had a look of irritation that marred her features. She was attractive, with short brown hair and steel gray eyes, and the sharpest mind Tamilya had ever encountered.

When it came out that the FBI might have had an opportunity to stop the bombing, everything had gone to shit. It had been Addie's job to oversee the investigation into the splinter group that had eventually blown up the Virginia Star Mall. Tamilya had been wondering if they were going to make her boss the scapegoat. She had been wrong.

"How is it that I'm the only one who is getting blamed? How about all the men up the chain of command you submitted reports to?"

"They said it was your job to keep in contact with your CI."

"You mean the one that was murdered a week before the hit? The one I couldn't get hold of because he was freaking dead? I gave them three targets. One of them was the mall."

"I know this sucks."

"You have *no* idea."

"Yes, I do. I've been through things like this before. You'll make it through. Just keep your head down and it will sort itself all out."

"It's different for you."

They both knew it was the truth. Addie was considered FBI royalty, a woman who had a father and three uncles with distinguished careers with the FBI. She also was white, which helped out the majority of the time. Tamilya had never had to deal with racism right to her face, but she knew there was always some jackass with a badge who hated her for her sex *and* her skin color.

"I know," Addie sighed as she rose out of her chair to walk around the desk and take the one next to Tamilya. "I am going to do everything I can to protect you, since the suspension is temporary."

"With pay?"

When Addie didn't say anything, Tamilya sighed. "I'm going to have to resign."

Sadness stole over Addie's features. "Don't."

"How long does one of these investigations take usually?" The sour look on her supervisor's face told her all she needed to know. "Right."

Tamilya looked around the office. When she had started this job, she had dreamed of one day having Addie's position. Up until seven days ago, she had been on track. But she couldn't go without a paycheck. She could last several months, but sometimes investigations could linger for a year. Without pay, she couldn't make it. The only way to survive would be to leave the job she loved. Her chest hurt as her head started to pound.

"Tamilya, don't do this. I need you here."

She studied her mentor, the woman who had hand-picked her out of the academy and had kept her at her side for all these years.

"I owe you, Addie. I know that. But, if they decide to make me a scapegoat, I'll lose any chance of making a career of this outside of the FBI. And I don't want it coming back on you." And she knew without a doubt, they would do it. When people above you made mistakes you warned them about, *you* paid the price.

She sighed. "No. I understand. I do know a few people you could hit up for a job, and you know I'll give you a recommendation."

"Thank you." She rose out of her chair, her heart even heavier than when she had walked into the office that morning. "I'll write up my resignation before I clean out my office."

"Remember, use me as a reference. I owe you that much."

"Thanks," she said, as she stepped out of the office and felt the attention of the entire group latch onto her. Everyone knew that she had been suspended by now. She wanted to hide, run away and pretend that the last ten days hadn't happened.

Instead, she did as her mother taught her. She raised her chin and ignored everyone as she walked to her office. She could hold it together until then…and she did. But the moment she shut the door, she leaned back against it, then sunk to the floor. There, in the privacy of her office, she felt the pain and sadness hit her. She knew it would take her weeks to recover from this, months...years even. She had spent her life planning for her career. And it was now gone. Granted, she could fight it; but, in the end, she only had about a twenty percent chance of winning that fight.

Before she did anything, she rested her forehead on her knees and let the tears fall.

Chapter One

Today was *not* going to suck.

At least, that's what Marcus Floyd was hoping. As he pulled his Task Force Hawaii shirt over his head and tucked it into his pants, he knew that it was probably just false hope. His work days had started sucking since Tamilya Lowe had been hired several months earlier.

It wasn't anything Tamilya had done. In fact, she had been above reproach, professional, and damned nicer than he deserved. Only the two of them knew exactly why she had every right to treat him as if he were the scum of the Earth. When he had blown up their relationship four years earlier, he should have known it would come back to bite him in the ass. They interacted when she was with the FBI and he worked with the Capital Police. Once she had left the FBI and he'd moved to Hawaii, he had thought he'd probably never see her again. She had started working with security contractors and, well…he'd been stupid enough to think that she'd never show up on Oahu. There was a reason for that.

He was a damned coward.

There was no other way to see it. He didn't want to face her. In fact, he was still upset about how he'd fucked up their relationship. So every time he saw her, Marcus had to deal with all of those thoughts—not to mention his attraction. He'd thought he was doing them both a favor when he'd stepped away from their affair, but now, he wasn't so sure. They still had the same chemistry and he was reminded about it, day after day. More than once he'd found himself fantasizing about the sound of her voice in the dark, or the way she would moan.

"Fuck," he muttered.

He felt the first stirrings of another erection. He'd already had to take care of himself in the shower, thanks to a vivid dream starring Tamilya. He closed his eyes, took a deep breath, and ordered his body to calm down. Every day, his attraction seemed to take over his better thoughts. He was close to making a fool of himself and that wasn't acceptable. Not in DC and not here in Hawaii.

The problem was, he couldn't avoid her. Since they were both experts in terrorism, they ended up spending a lot of time together. Before she joined the team, he would get breathers between their meetings, but now he saw her at least five days a week. And damn, she was more beautiful and amazing with each passing day. Resisting the urge to steal a kiss was getting harder and harder, but they worked together on the team. He didn't want to step over that line.

Although, damn, it might be worth it if she was still attracted to him. They hadn't just had good sex. They'd had the most amazing sex of his life. If he could have one more chance to get her back under him...or on top of him...

Fuck. There he went again. He drew in a breath and calmed himself once again. There was no way she would have anything to do with him. That ship had sailed a long time ago.

He walked into the living room, grabbed his coffee, and stepped out on his balcony. The first thing he smelled were the plumeria. It permeated the air frequently in the mornings, especially when there was a little bit of rain. He'd heard it tapping against his window this morning, and that is what had actually pulled him from his erotic dream starring Tamilya.

His apartment was small, and more than a little over-priced, but he liked the view. There was nothing in the world like watching the sun rise over Diamond Head. Whenever he had a chance, he made sure to catch it. He gave up a few nights out to eat and space he probably didn't even need for this luxury. He'd learned the hard way that it was important to enjoy the little things.

His phone buzzed and he glanced at the screen. The selfie he took with his mother last time she visited popped up.

He clicked on his phone because avoiding his mother would have dire consequences.

"Good morning," he said.

"Good morning to you too. I didn't call too early, did I?" his mother asked. She lived on the East coast and had a hell of a time remembering the time difference when he had first relocated to Hawaii.

"Naw. We had a call last night, but thankfully, I wasn't on duty."

"Good. I have news," she said, her voice shimmering with excitement. "I wanted to let you know that Viv is getting married."

"Ken finally got the nerve to ask her?"

His sister's boyfriend had asked Marcus for permission to ask her to marry him about three months ago. Granted, Marcus thought it was stupid to have to ask a man to marry a female family member. One thing his life in the house of women had taught him was that women were definitely smarter and stronger than any man. Viv didn't need permission to marry from anyone but herself.

"Yes. I don't know why that boy took so long. I think Viv has known for a little while, and I have a feeling you did too. You don't sound surprised."

No way was he telling his mother about Ken asking him. She'd probably boycott the wedding in protest. His mother did a lot of protesting in public and with their family.

"I just had a feeling. The guy has been hung up on her for eight years. I just assumed it was coming soon."

"Okay." She didn't sound like she believed him, but then his mother wasn't a dummy. There was a good chance he'd end up paying for it later. "Anyway, they were thinking that they wanted to keep it small."

"Really? Viv wants a small wedding?" He couldn't keep the skepticism out of his voice. There was one thing he knew about his sister and that was she did not do anything in a small way. Loud, funny, irreverent, and thoroughly lovable, she always garnered attention in any group.

"Small, because she wants to do a destination wedding."

"Destination wedding? Are we *that* family? Do we have that kind of money?"

His mother was a college professor, so she was definitely comfortable, but a wedding at one of those destination places was expensive, even if there were only a few people attending.

"We don't need it. Viv and Ken have it." That much was true. They both worked as engineers on things too complicated for Marcus to understand, and they both made top dollar.

"Where is this destination, and how much time am I going to have to take off for it?"

"Not much because they want to do it in Hawaii."

He grunted. "That's good."

"Yes, I'm sure we're all worried about your time schedule," she said, sarcasm dripping from every word. "Anyway, I wanted to tell you before she calls."

"Why?"

"Marcus, you and I both know you love your sisters, but you tend to be a negative Ned when talking about things like weddings."

"No one would ever call me Ned."

"Stop that. Just, be nice when she calls."

"I promise. Is that all you called for?"

"Mostly. But it's not like I need a reason to call my baby boy."

Considering that her baby boy was now six foot three and weighed over two hundred pounds, he assumed his mother was never going to give up calling him her baby. So he ignored it.

"So, it was mostly because of Viv." Marcus knew needling his mother was a safe activity with thousands of miles between them.

"Don't sound like that. I also want to know how work is going."

"Going okay. Looks like Del is going to add more people, or so the rumor goes."

"And have you been seeing anyone?"

Damn, he shouldn't have pushed her. His mother wanted them all married off and happy, and she constantly worried about him being all alone out there in Hawaii. She acted like he didn't have an active social life. He did. In fact, this past weekend he'd gone fishing with Adam.

Damn.

"Haven't really had time."

"Hmm," was her only response.

He knew it well and understood she didn't believe him. One thing he hated about Hawaii was being so far from his family, but it was also one of the better things. If he was still living on the mainland, both his sisters and his mother would be after him about dating. Jessika constantly tried to fix him up with the other high-powered attorneys she worked with, and it always ended in disaster. They talked down to him like he was stupid, and he got pissed off and barely paid attention to them after that.

"Listen, I have a feeling that only a few of us are going to be making it in this morning because of the call last night, so I need to get a move on."

"You can run but you can't hide from me, Marcus," she said with a chuckle. "Be careful."

"I will. Love you, Mom."

"Love you."

He clicked off his phone and sat down in one of the two chairs he kept on the balcony. He did need to get into work, but first, he was going to sip his Kona and watch the sun rise. The first pink and purple rays peeked out over Diamond Head signaling the true beginning of the day.

He had a few things on his plate, and he was sure there would be something on the dead body from this morning. And then there was his original worry of the morning: Tamilya. It seemed that he had been thinking of her more and more lately, and he needed to stop it. That bridge had been burned a long time ago, and there was no use rehashing what went wrong. Marcus knew there was no going back to what was, but at least they could work together. He would just have to be happy with that.

And, if he lusted after her in his dreams, he would deal with it. At some point, he would

simply have to move on.

———

"DAMMIT," Tamilya muttered. She poked herself in the eye for the second time that morning while applying her makeup. Blinking, she grabbed a tissue and dabbed at the marks beneath her eye. Normally, it took her just a few minutes to slap on her makeup and run out the door, but today was different.

She knew the reason. *Marcus Floyd.*

They were the two who had been off last night, so more than likely, they would handle any calls that would come in to TFH today. Most people would think she was insane to work with her ex, but they seemed to handle it better than most. Sure, every time he said her name, she had to fight a shiver. He had one of those deep baritones that tumbled over the syllables of her name. And that made her an idiot because she had been there and done that and had been left with a broken heart when he ran out the door.

With a sigh, she pushed those thoughts away and focused on getting ready for work. Thankfully, she didn't have to spend time on her hair. About six months earlier, she stopped with the extensions and flat irons and the like. She loved the way her natural hair looked on her and while she had to do some maintenance on it, it was nothing like the pain in the ass it had been previously. It had been a freeing experience.

She cleaned up her face, poured more coffee into her travel mug, then stood in front of the mirror to take a quick check of her attire. She studied her outfit for the day. The power suits were a thing of the past. Now, she could wear jeans and short sleeved shirts, and—thank the baby Jesus—comfortable shoes. She didn't mind heels when she was socializing, but even the most comfortable low heels didn't compare to wearing her short boots.

She nodded her head, then grabbed her phone and keys before heading out for the day. The moment she opened the door, the sweet Hawaiian air wrapped around her. She knew that many people liked the sunsets, but she had always been a morning person. And there was nothing like the air at the break of dawn in Hawaii. Maybe there was, but Tamilya had never experienced it.

As she turned the corner, she saw her father. Okay, so she didn't own her little house next to the ocean in Hawaii. It was the in-law suite her parents had in their backyard. It wasn't uncommon for families in Hawaii to live like this due to the housing shortage and the pricing, but it was usually the other way around, with the retired parents living in what was essentially a pool house. Still, it was better than that townhouse she owned in Virginia. Just walking to her car left her freezing the rest of the day. Nowadays, she had her mother's home cooking, time with her father, and private pool she could use any day of the week.

"Good morning, sweetheart," her father said as he sat

down on the edge of the pool and dipped his legs into the water. Another benefit of the house was living close to her parents. Her father had been an executive with one of the top construction companies in the Southeast when he'd had his heart attack a few years ago. After that, her parents had packed up everything and moved back to Hawaii. She'd thought they were crazy until she visited them. After that, she worked to get transferred here with Dillon Securities.

She'd been on island for close to two years, and each day, she fell a little more in love with it.

"Morning, Dad," she said leaning down to kiss his cheek.

He was in his trunks, but he was still wearing his top, albeit unbuttoned. Anyone looking at him would think he was in peak health, that nothing had ever gotten close to killing him. That is until you saw the scars on his chest from his surgery.

"Running late?" he asked.

"A little."

"Did you eat?"

She shook her head. "I'll grab something on the way. We had a body come in last night, and I have paperwork I need to finish before we have the briefing on that."

He nodded. "Tell your mother you ate. She worries."

"I will if I see her."

She leaned down and kissed his cheek.

"Be good, Tamilya."

"I always am."

"Tamilya?"

She turned and waited.

"You're happy, right? You don't mind living here, do you?"

She walked toward him. "No. Why?"

He shrugged. "I was just thinking this morning that your talents are wasted here. I know you came here because of us."

"In fact, with the rise of cyber terrorism from Russia and China, along with some militant religious groups, Hawaii is in a unique position. They have a lot more threats than people think."

"But you're not working for the FBI."

"No. I'm working with them on a few things. Along with my contacts in the military and ATF, I have a wide range of different organizations to deal with. It's much more interesting than the job I had when I worked at the Bureau."

"You're sure?"

She nodded, even though a tiny bit of her always would mourn her FBI career, dead as it was. She had never really loved it the way she loved the TFH job. From their unique cases to her coworkers, she had found her place. Then there was the biggest benefit of all: her parents.

"Besides, the real reason for being here is to be with you and Mom."

"You're a sweet girl."

"I know. Mom tells me I get that from her."

He chuckled again and she felt her mood lighten. Having her father safe and alive was more important to her than even her career.

"Besides, it was eleven degrees in DC this morning and I wasn't there for that."

He chuckled. "I told you that you weren't built for DC weather."

It was true. She had spent a chunk of her life moving

around, but most of her life had been in the South. There was no hiding that fact with her accent, that was for sure. However, she also couldn't handle the weather. She loved snow, but she didn't appreciate living in a place where it snowed on a regular basis. She liked the mild winters in Florida a lot better than the snowmaggdens that tended to land on DC.

"Be good today, Dad," she said, before leaving him to his coffee. She knew that he would spend a few minutes there, enjoying the beginning of the day. Tamilya's heart always squeezed tight when she thought about almost losing him a few years ago.

She really didn't have time to stop off and talk with her mother, but she knew if she didn't, Diane Lowe would never let her hear the end of it.

"Good morning, sweetie," her mother said as Tamilya stepped through the door.

"Morning, Mom."

Her mother was holding a muffin up. "Take, eat, and I will pretend that you are actually eating right."

"I am most of the time. Living in Hawaii makes that easy."

"I told you. Will you be home for dinner?"

She shrugged. "I know we caught a murder last night, but I have a feeling it won't have anything to do with me. I'll text you and let you know."

She kissed her mom on the cheek. "Love ya."

"Love you back," she said as Tamilya hurried out the door. It was a Godsend living with her parents. She made good money, but even with decent pay, she would probably have to live in an apartment. She didn't mind, but she also liked living in her little cottage with access to a pool. That being said, living in Kailua, she had a long drive every morning. Since she was running late, she was sure to hit heavy traffic.

With a sigh, she slipped into her car and backed out of the drive. Nothing like starting the week off right by being late to work.

Chapter Two

"Dammit," Tamilya muttered as pain radiated from her forehead. She'd been reading her texts and walked into the door that lead into Task Force Hawaii.

She stumbled back and regained her balance with the help of strong male hands. She knew those hands and just what they could do to her body. His scent hit her next. He always used the same kind of soap, which lingered on his flesh, but it was different these days. That masculine scent was there, but it seemed to intermingle with the sweet Hawaiian air. Whatever it was, it made Tamilya want to snuggle up close to him and get lost in the scent.

"Whoa, Tammy," Marcus said, his breath against her cheek.

Her heart rate ticked up, her blood warmed, and hell, her nipples tightened. No matter how much she resented the fact, her body responded to Marcus. She counted down from ten...then counted again two more times before she spoke.

"Thanks," she muttered, hearing the arousal she couldn't quite hide.

He hesitated for just a second, and her pulse stuttered for that one little moment. Then, he let her go. He was probably just trying to make sure she didn't fall down. He had made it damned clear that a longer relationship did not interest him. She couldn't let him know that she wanted him more now than she had four years ago. That would make her kind of pathetic. And it seemed her day wasn't going to get any better.

"Are you sure you're okay?" he asked, his low voice soft.

She nodded and mentally girded her loins before she looked at him. Even prepared, she felt the rush of heat and the embarrassment of their past relationship. The man might have moved to Hawaii and, like the rest of them, dressed more casually, but it didn't diminish his power. He wore one of the dark blue polo shirts with the TFH emblem and jeans. He should have the same effect that all of the other men in their unit had on her, which was no effect whatsoever. Maybe it was because she knew what he looked like naked.

"Tamilya?"

She blinked and realized she had been standing there thinking about him being naked. Again. Her face heated and she cleared her throat.

"Yeah, I was just reading a report and did what I bitch at other people for doing."

He chuckled and she fought the temptation to touch him. Most women melted at the chuckle and definitely after being touched by Marcus. The man had a reputation and Tamilya had seen the looks from other women. Worse, she knew what it sounded like in the dark.

"How are your sisters doing?"

She smiled, happy for the distractions. "They're fine.

Bethany just got accepted into Harvard Law and Sondra is on her way to Quantico."

"Following in her sister's footsteps."

"Let's hope not," she muttered as she opened the door to TFH and tried to ignore the rock in her belly that always appeared when her career with the FBI came up. She had left in a cloud of suspicion and embarrassment. The fact that she had landed a job with Dillon Security, which then led to TFH, had been a Godsend.

It was quiet in the headquarters, especially this early in the morning. She knew that they had a call out the night before, one that she had been happy to miss. A dead body at two in the morning was not her thing. She could do the work, but she had always been considered a terrorism expert, and that was where she felt most comfortable. But as part of the team, she sometimes had to handle those calls as well. Thankfully, she hadn't been on call last evening.

She saw TJ Callahan, FBI agent and husband to TFH's forensics expert Charity, talking to their boss. Whatever it was, it was serious. TJ was frowning as he spoke.

"Do you know what he's here for?" she asked.

"Probably has something to do with the DB last night. Might have an FBI connection. Or, he's avoiding work."

She snorted. The Hammer—his nickname due to the fact that his parents had named him Thor—didn't screw around, and he was wearing a suit, so he was definitely going into the work. The agent noticed Tamilya and Marcus and must have said something to Del because he turned around, then motioned with his hand.

"And we have been summoned," Marcus said with a smile in his voice.

No one resented Del. She knew many people hated their boss, but Del was a different kind of guy. She'd worked with men who treated her like an idiot. Del was always respectful of every woman in TFH, especially his wife Emma, who had a genius IQ.

She walked to the door and TJ opened it just as she reached it.

"Morning," he said. He glanced at Marcus, then back to her. TJ knew their history, as did everyone else in the office. She could see the calculation in his eyes. He saw the two of them coming in together—except they hadn't been together, unfortunately.

Dammit. No, Tamilya. Stop daydreaming about the walking heartbreak Marcus Floyd.

"Morning. What are you doing here?" she asked, happy that her voice actually sounded normal.

"It has to do with the body from this morning," Del said as she stepped into the office. "He has a tie to the FBI."

She got a good look at Del and remembered he had been on call last night. Unlike the others, though, he hadn't been home yet. She knew that because there were dark circles under his eyes and his hair…well, it needed a good brushing.

"A tie?" Marcus asked.

"Yeah. We've identified him as Andrei Golubev," Del said.

The name had her blood running cold as she looked at TJ. "Golubev? I thought he was dead."

"That was our doing," TJ said. "Well, not mine, but someone had him spilling secrets for the FBI. The man had a lot of information and evidence to back it all up."

The ramifications of what he'd just disclosed hit her

hard. A dead Russian who had apparently been in FBI protection giving them secrets? Damn. This wasn't just a little screw up. This was definite a FUBAR situation.

"Jesus, TJ, that is a big screw up," Tamilya said.

"Who is this guy?" Marcus asked.

TJ didn't say anything, so she filled Marcus in on the guy.

"He wasn't a big player, but more like a lackey with money. Putin used to call him his favorite little runt—or whatever the Russian expression was for it—because he was just a little over five foot and not that attractive. He would also do anything to make Putin happy. And you all faked his death? Did you tell the CIA?"

"Again, not my decision. And, to the best of my knowledge, no, they didn't tell them."

"Damn, TJ, the CIA is not going to be happy. They are going to crucify you in the press and any congressional hearings."

He shrugged. "That's for someone at a higher pay grade to handle."

"So someone leaked to Russia that he was cooperating?" Marcus asked.

"That's our best bet. He had no family left. Not married, no parents or siblings."

"That's not the problem," Del said. "Tell them."

TJ grimaced. "We didn't know he was in Hawaii. Actually, no one knew where he was."

It just got worse and worse by the minute. The ramifications were hitting her. "And we're just finding out about this?" she asked.

"He had no ties here, so it doesn't make sense that he would show up here."

"He simply disappeared and there was no warning?" Marcus asked.

TJ opened his mouth to argue, but Tamilya stopped him.

"If he were missing, and even if they knew it, they wouldn't throw out the name for a while. They would want to try their damndest to keep it under wraps. Telling people they were looking for him would alert Russian authorities, especially if the FSB got hold of it. He's got to have the goods on some of the most powerful people in Russia. If they truly thought he was dead, the FBI would want to keep it out of the media."

"We're not the media," Del said.

She shrugged. "Any kind of leak could be bad. The Bear is everywhere," she said, referencing one of the many Cold War slogans spies used. Russia was known as the Bear. Their ability to buy off people was legendary. "There's a good chance Golubev just went on a bender."

"Really?" Del asked.

"Yeah. When I was with the FBI, he had a reputation that always worried his Russian handlers. He liked women, a lot of them, the flashier the better. He was also a drunk, and he couldn't seem to keep his money in the bank. He would spend it as fast as he earned it. If it was big and expensive, he wanted it. He earned fortunes several times just to screw them away. Literally."

"And that's a problem?" Marcus asked.

"Of course. You know the issues with someone in debt. They are ripe for being bought by the wrong people. I know people in the military who didn't get high security jobs because of their debt. Also, his need for women to love him would definitely open him up to a honey pot kind of job."

Sending in someone to seduce a spy just didn't happen in the movies. The honey pot scheme was used by every spy organization in the world.

"There's panic in the FBI right now because they don't know where the leak is," TJ said.

"I can imagine," Marcus said. As usual, there was a thread of disdain in his voice. Marcus had a real hatred for the FBI these days, and she didn't know why. He hadn't shown it when they worked together in DC.

"Okay, what do you want from us?" she asked.

"TFH has better contacts on the ground. You can ask around without causing too many problems. I show up with my haole face and they're going to know I'm FBI."

Marcus snorted. "It's not like Tammy and I won't have the same problem."

Del's attention shifted from Marcus to her. She knew he caught the change in her name, but their boss said nothing. It wasn't like they had hidden their past relationship, but he had never used that particular nickname for her since they'd split up. Until this morning.

"I figured you could have Adam help, but don't give me that kind of bullshit. I know both of you and I know you have the contacts," TJ said.

She could see that Marcus was raring up to argue with TJ. What she didn't understand was why. She knew he liked TJ, but for some reason, this request was sticking in his craw. They didn't have time for that though. Not if they had someone running around Hawaii killing off operatives.

"First of all, we have no idea why he was here. More than likely he followed a woman because he had no issues with being led around by his dick."

"I thought you were the gentler sex?" Del asked, humor lacing his words.

She rolled her eyes. "It could have been chance. It could have been a meet up. Marcus and I can sniff around, but if you take down a ring, TFH gets partial credit. It's that or we don't help you."

TJ rocked back on his heels. "Anything. The FBI would do anything to get this situated without any kind of media."

"We aren't the ones who have an issue with leaks," Marcus said.

"True. Okay, I'll shoot all three of you the information. I'll continue to be the POC as usual."

"We need access to the crime scene. Do we still have that?" Marcus asked.

"Yeah," TJ said.

"We'll keep you informed," Del said rising from behind his desk. Both she and Marcus stayed seated. Del would definitely want to talk this out. It took a few minutes to finish up with TJ, then he rejoined them in his office, closing the door behind him.

"Alright, what are your first thoughts?" he asked, directing the question to Tamilya.

"As I said, I knew of him. The CIA tried numerous times to turn him, so they would probably be pissed if they knew the FBI had him."

"The letter agencies are a bunch of bitchy little whiners," Marcus said.

"True, but we are a letter agency," she said with a smile. "It could be as I said. He came here with a woman and someone saw him."

"How often does that actually happen?" Del asked.

"A lot more than you'd think. We had someone who had turned an oligarch from Russia who had turned on Putin. Mainly because we caught him outside of Russia supplying illegal arms. He was seen at a resort by an FSB agent on vacation. He was dead within forty-eight hours. That is one of many. These guys are good at making money, but they are sometimes so damned arrogant it leads to their deaths."

"Maybe that was it and the person who killed him is gone," Del said. He sighed. "Knowing our luck…"

"Right," Marcus said. He looked at her. "You going to do some calling around?"

She nodded as she saw TFH's second-in-command Adam Lee walk into the main office. "There's Adam, can you talk to him while I dig around with my contacts?"

He nodded.

"Good," Del said. "I'm really thankful we have both of you. This is making me twitchy, and I like that I have the two of you with your particular backgrounds."

"Does that mean we get a raise?" Marcus asked as he held the door open for her.

"I'll give you one when I get one. Keep me updated."

"Will do, boss," Marcus said. "Do you want this opened or closed?"

"Closed. I need to get ready for this interview today."

"I didn't know you were adding to the team," she said.

"They're talking about expanding our duties. If they do that, I need more people. We're already strained."

She nodded and turned as Adam walked up to them. "We're doing the grunt work for the FBI?" he asked.

"Yeah," Marcus answered. "I hate the idea of dealing with them, but if we have someone killing assets on our turf, then we need to stop him. We're going to be better at it than the FBI."

"Speaking of the FBI, I need to call around," she said.

"Addie?" Marcus asked, his tone flat. She didn't know what he had against her old boss in the FBI, but it started about the same time as his disdain for the organization.

"Yes. Is there a problem?"

He shook his head. "Adam and I can start making a list of people to talk to."

"Let me grab some coffee first," Adam said as he left to do just that.

Marcus nodded.

"Seriously, Marcus, what *is* your problem with Addie?" she asked.

"None."

She knew he wasn't telling her the truth, but she let it go. They didn't need to get into any kind of fight when they had so much work ahead of them. "I'll get to work since I know some of my contacts will be heading to bed soon."

She headed to her office, trying her best not to growl. She was excited about the opportunity, but working with Marcus on something like this wasn't going to be fun.

When she had first gotten hired by TFH, she didn't know if she could be more than civil to him. Their relationship had been over before either of them could blink. It wasn't only that he ended it. It was that he thought she would fall apart when he'd dumped her.

But these last few months had proven the two of them could work together. Of course, she still had issues with the occasional dream. She had no control over her subconscious, and she had been going through a dry spell.

Here she was, sitting in her office like some teenager with a crush on her teacher. She shook herself and then grabbed her phone. It was time to start making those calls. Daydreaming about a man like Marcus Floyd only led to heartache.

Chapter Three

Tamilya took a calming breath and tried to get her nerves under control. She'd been working with TFH for a few months now, and while they'd had a few terrorism issues, nothing quite this big had hit them. This was going to be something big. She felt down to her bones.

She sat down and tried to get her thoughts in order before she called Addie. Knowing her old boss, she already knew what was happening. Even when things happened in other divisions, Addie always seemed to know what was going on. Tamilya rolled her shoulders trying to ease the tension there. She knew she always held it there and any time she talked to Addie, it returned.

In the years since she left the FBI, she began to understand what had happened there and why having Addie for a boss was probably a bad idea. Addie presented herself as a team player. She was damned good at her job and her info was always spot on. But when it came to anyone else's career, she would happily throw them under the bus. She'd learned that the hard way and when she had started working for Dillon Securities, she had been uncomfortable with sharing much of herself outside of work with Conner Dillon. Bit by bit, Conner had pulled her out of her shell. She owed him for that.

Now the crew at TFH would never allow her to stand-offish. It was impossible. They just wouldn't let her keep to herself.

She smiled and used that warm feeling she got from working with TFH to ground her. She needed to use that when she talked to Addie. If not, Addie would pick up on her irritation. There was nothing that would ever convince Tamilya that Addie didn't use her as a scapegoat.

With a sigh, she pushed those thoughts aside. She would focus on the task at hand and the fact that she didn't have to deal with the FBI on a regular basis.

She hit Addie's number in her contacts, and she picked up on the first ring.

"Hey, there. I was wondering when you would be calling."

———

MARCUS POURED himself a coffee and offered the pot to Adam. He shook his head and took a sip. He'd already been nursing his cup of coffee for a few minutes now.

"Are you sure you don't want some more? You look like crap."

Adam looked worse than Del; although, he did appear somewhat more refreshed. His clothes weren't wrinkled but the dark circles under his eyes were more prominent. Probably because he'd been home and Del hadn't.

"No, thanks. I have a little paperwork to file, then I'm heading home. I'll never get any sleep if I drink any more coffee than this."

Marcus nodded. "And you're saved from handling this case."

"Not really. We're all going to be on deck because of the national security issues."

"True," Marcus said as he sipped his coffee. The smooth Kona brew slid down his throat. Inwardly he sighed. For a decade, he drank the crap cop coffee, so getting good coffee at work was a blessing. It was one of the many reasons he loved working at TFH.

"So, you and Tamilya will be working together," Adam said.

At first, Marcus didn't catch onto the tone, but then it hit him. He glanced up at Adam and saw that idiotic smile.

"Yeah. Like we always do on things like this." Adam didn't say anything, but his smile widened into a grin. "What?"

"This is different."

"No. It's not."

And if he said it enough, he might just remember that it was just the job. He'd slipped up twice today and called her Tammy. It was the name he had used when they were dating, but he knew no one else used it. It was somehow more intimate than her given name, and he had best not use it again. Today, for some reason, he couldn't stop calling her that.

"Whatever you say, Bruddah," Adam said with a chuckle.

"Just lay off, Adam." All of a sudden it hit him. If Adam had noticed the tension, the other idiots they worked with would too. That meant one thing. "I want you to make sure there are no bets. Tamilya wouldn't like it."

"Oh, so you're worried about her feelings?"

"She wouldn't like it." He repeated it like a mantra. Truthfully, it was more about him than Tamilya. She had a good sense of humor, but he was worried it would make it impossible for him to get her back.

Whoa. He didn't want that. Didn't need that. The two of them just didn't work. Not back in DC and definitely not now that they worked together here in Hawaii. When she had first arrived in Hawaii, he had entertained getting back with her. But he knew what she wanted, and Marcus wasn't built for that. He lusted after her on a daily basis, but he also had tremendous respect for her. He'd realized when she'd started at TFH that he couldn't put both of them through that breakup mess again.

Adam crossed his arms over his massive chest. "Is that a fact?"

No matter what he said, Marcus knew it would be taken the wrong way. "Get bent, Adam."

Adam threw his head back and laughed. "You're such an easy target."

Marcus tried to ignore him and hoped it would go away, but, as with everything in TFH, that would not be the end of it. Autumn Bradford, the ex-DEA agent Del hired around the same time as Tamilya, stepped out of her office with a quizzical look on her face.

"What's so funny?"

"Nothing," Marcus said.

"Marcus and Tamilya have to work together on a case."

Autumn looked at Marcus with her eyebrows raised. "Really?"

"We've worked together these last few months. I don't know why everyone is so freaked out about it."

Autumn took a sip of her coffee and studied him. When she did this—and she did it a lot—he always felt like a specimen in a lab. It wasn't just the way she looked at him. He'd seen her look at everyone that way, including suspects. He knew her social skills were unique after being raised in a cult, but it was unsettling when she lasered in on him. Now he knew why she was such a good interrogator. He was ready to tell her anything she wanted as long as she quit staring at him.

"Well, because you got it bad for the woman."

He wanted to growl but that would make Adam laugh. Again.

"I didn't ask your opinion."

"Yes you did. You said you didn't know why everyone was so freaked out about it. We're intrigued because you two had a very short, intense relationship."

He wanted to just walk into his office, slam the door, and ignore them both. There were two reasons he couldn't do that. One was that it would prove their point, but the second was how Autumn described their relationship.

"How do you know it was short and intense?"

It had been, but it wasn't like he'd told anyone the details. Had Tamilya? He knew Tamilya and Autumn had hit it off since they knew a lot of the same people.

"Well, if it had been long and then died out, there wouldn't be all this heat between you. If it had been long and intense, you would still be angry. So, short, intense, and incomplete."

He hated that she was so close to the truth. At least she didn't know that he had been the idiot to walk away. Or at least, he hoped she didn't. He knew there were a few people wondering, but he was the only one who knew what an ass he had been. Assuming that just because she had said she loved him and that she wanted happily ever after was stupid. He'd panicked and run. Within a few days, he had known he'd made a huge mistake, but she refused to give in. She hadn't been mean about it. Worse, she had been politely dismissive. The woman could cut glass with her tone.

"How do you know all this?" he asked.

Autumn shrugged. "I'm good at reading people. Kind of important when your father is a whacked out of his mind cult leader."

Her father had run a cult on the Big Island. He knew a little about it, but mostly that he was running guns and drugs through the entire camp. He had been the biggest supplier of Ice on that island for years. Not to mention his issues with having ten or so wives, most of them under the age of fifteen. He couldn't even imagine what it had been like for her. Her escape had been the downfall of her father.

"It also helped when I worked undercover with the DEA."

"I didn't know you did that," he said. He had known she was in the DEA, but he had no idea she had been undercover. People who excelled at that—and he had no reason not to think she excelled—were always a little on edge. They had to play a delicate balancing act between the worlds of law enforcement and the drug business.

She offered him a toothy grin and, not for the first time, he thought she was younger than her thirty years. She looked like she'd just graduated from college.

"I was really good at it. I can play the space cadet and people buy into it. They always thought I was stupid. Taking them down was damned satisfying."

He smiled, enjoying her bloodthirsty tone. He could

understand it. When he did a little undercover work, he always liked letting racists think he was stupid.

"If you liked it so much, why did you leave?"

She sighed. "UC work has its drawbacks." Then she didn't elaborate, but that was par for the course for her. She could dig under anyone's skin, but no one had really cracked her. He would know because it was impossible to keep secrets in the TFH Ohana.

Tamilya stepped out of her office and for a second, he couldn't think. She was dressed all in black. Dark jeans and t-shirt, along with black boots, which made her look like a badass. The gun on her hip and the sunglasses he knew she would put on the moment they stepped outside made her close to irresistible. She used to wear her hair straight with extensions, but since starting to work with TFH, she'd gone natural. It didn't matter what she did with her hair or how she dressed, he would always want her. He knew that would never change, but he wasn't sure on how to go about getting another chance with her.

Dammit, no. He didn't want another chance. Wrong. He shouldn't want another chance, and he definitely didn't deserve one anyway.

Find a way.

Jesus. He had to stop thinking those things or he would start thinking they had a chance. And they didn't. Mostly.

"Earth to Marcus," Adam said snapping his fingers.

"What?" He turned and found both Adam and Autumn staring at him with curiosity. They were both smiling.

"You want to shoot me the list of your contacts?" he asked.

"Sure, and I can call up an old CI who might know something about the murder."

"Thanks. You might want to shoot that info to TJ as well."

Adam nodded, still smiling.

"What?"

"I just think you both have issues still."

Issues? That sounded too simple for their relationship, but he would rather die than admit it to Adam. "And?"

"Just saying what I was thinking," Adam said.

"Hey, what's up?" Tamilya asked.

"Nothing. Did you get hold of Addie?" Marcus asked.

"Yeah. She's sending what she knows about the op. She's actually on her way out the door."

"For the day?"

"No. She's retiring. Got some big job with that Jansen and Associates. She's only going to be at the FBI until the end of next week."

He said nothing else. He didn't like the woman and never would. During their time together, and actually before that when they'd just been friends, Marcus thought Tamilya's supervisor took advantage of her. Addie was smart, but Tamilya was smarter and definitely more capable. He'd never seen an FBI agent so young whose instincts were so well developed. He'd kept his thoughts to himself until she threw Tamilya to the wolves. *That* was unforgivable.

"Did you have some people we can hunt up?" she asked Adam.

He nodded. "Yeah. I shot the list to you both."

"Good, you can go over them because you're better at that," Marcus said. "And I want to stop by the hotel. If they're holding the room for us to look over, I want to do that before they revoke the privilege. Elle is working on the autopsy, so we should have those results when we get back."

She slanted him a look as her lips turned down. "But that means you're driving."

He frowned. "Yeah."

"Fine, but don't put any Willie Nelson on today. I'm not in the mood," she said brushing past him as she made her way to the door.

"Ah, but every day is a good day when Willie is singing."

She muttered something under her breath, and he smiled. She might be irritated with him, but spending the day with Tamilya was better than a day without her. Even if she was ticked off at him.

"Text if you need us for anything," he said to Adam and followed Tamilya out of the office. He had no problem walking behind her. She had a sassy little sway to her hips that he always enjoyed. It matched the sass in her voice. She'd spent most of her childhood in the South and it was clearly evident in her voice. It was another thing they had in common.

"Did Addie have any ideas?"

She shook her head. "She's really out of the loop on this one. Since it was an op that would continue on for a while after she retired, she didn't have anything to do with interrogating Golubev."

"Makes sense," he said, holding the door open for her. He waited for her to walk outside and slip on those sunglasses. He bit back a sigh. Definite badass.

"Yeah, the Middle East is more her area. She did say that the blame game was in full swing. Almost as bad as after the Virginia Star Mall bombing. I think she was enjoying that a bit."

"Why? It's not like she took a hit on that."

She stopped walking. "What do you mean?"

He turned to face her. He didn't want this conversation. Not now. Not ever. Marcus got irrationally angry whenever he thought about Addie.

"Marcus?" she asked, settling her hands on her hips.

With a sigh, he said, "She should have protected you."

"It wouldn't have done any good. Besides, I would probably have been in DC this week, and they've got twelve inches of snow. This," she said motioning with her hands, "is ten times better than any snowmageden."

He chuckled. "You got me there. Sometimes I think I miss it, then I talk to a friend still working for the Capitol Police and I think...maybe I'll just sit on the beach today."

She started walking again. "Yeah. Makes it even nicer since my folks are here."

"I don't know why I didn't know your folks lived here before."

"You never asked."

There was no anger behind her words, just a statement of fact. It was kind of sad how little they knew about each other. They had practically lived with each other for six weeks, but in the six months since she arrived at TFH, he had learned so much more.

"Do you think we should hit the hotel room first?" she asked.

"Yeah, that way we can give Adam time to get hold of a few of his contacts; although, I still think this is someone from off island."

"Why do you say that?"

"You think they have someone waiting here?" Marcus asked.

"As I said before, the Bear is everywhere, but they also have no problem hiring out."

"That's true. Hopefully, we can get some answers from these people Adam knows."

He started up his vehicle and the music blared out of the speakers. He had been listening to Willie Nelson's channel this morning—as he usually did.

She groaned and covered her ears. "Oh my God. How did we ever date?"

He turned the music down and shot a grin in her direction. "It was my charming personality."

She lowered her hands and snorted.

"What?" he asked.

She shook her head.

"No. Tell me."

She sighed and glanced at him. "You think our whole relationship was about you."

"I didn't say that."

"Whatever," she said, dismissing him and looking out of the window while he pulled out of the parking place and into traffic.

It honestly stuck in his craw that she would think that about him. He had been obsessed since the first day he had met her on the job. She'd been FBI and he was in the Capital Police. They worked together on a joint terrorism task force and the moment she had smiled at him, he'd fallen for her.

"Our relationship was not all about me, and I didn't think it was."

"I know you like to rehash this like we were on a Housewives reunion show with Andy Cohen, but I think for the sake of our sanity, we should leave this alone. Especially since we have this crap to deal with. Taking our eyes off the ball could end badly for everyone involved. Ask the guys who didn't keep track of Golubev."

He smiled. "Fine. But some day, we need to talk this out."

"One thing I learned was that what you think we need and what I'm willing to give are completely at odds."

He wanted to argue more about it, but he knew she had been right. They had important things to work on, and one thing neither of them did was bring their personal issues to the job. He knew they probably didn't have a romantic future, but there was a tiny part of him that knew they needed to talk things over. Maybe then, there wouldn't be this tension between them.

And maybe he would be able to stop having erotic dreams about her…just maybe.

ADAM WATCHED Tamilya and Marcus walk out of view and his smile faded. They didn't have a policy of people dating at TFH, as long as no one was involved with a supervisor. Since Del was married, and Adam—well, he wanted someone who couldn't commit—they were okay on that front. He still worried every time two of them started a relationship, that it would affect the team.

"I got twenty on this weekend," Autumn said from behind him. He turned and found her texting furiously. "You want in?"

"I swear the boss said no more betting."

"So…that's a no?" she asked without looking up.

He sighed. "Leave me out of it so I can pretend I had no idea."

She laughed. "Okay. Are we having a staff meeting today?"

"I'm not sure, let me talk to Del and I'll let you know. It's probably off because the body from last night is the assignment Marcus and Tamilya got."

"Okay."

She turned and walked back to her office without saying anything else. She was a good agent, but she was a little…different. That was the best way to describe her. Considering her childhood, he considered her fairly normal.

"Adam," Del called out.

He turned and found his boss waving him into his office. Adam joined him.

"I guess Marcus filled you in?"

Adam nodded. "Sounds like a mess."

"Yeah and the Feds want to drop it in our laps."

"Then take the credit for it."

"Nope. Tamilya made sure to get an agreement to share the collar if we figure it out. Hopefully, they won't be dicks about it."

Adam nodded.

"I picked up on something," Del said carefully.

"What?" he asked.

"You don't think they're still involved, do you?"

"Marcus and Tamilya?" Adam asked.

Del nodded.

"I don't think so, why?"

"Just something odd this morning. And he called her Tammy."

"Tammy? Didn't she threaten to smack Carino if he called her Tammy?" Adam asked, mentioning their HPD liaison.

Del nodded. "Yeah. It was just…there was a vibe between them."

He had caught it too, but he didn't want to assume anything. It could be that there would always be that energy between them. "I really don't think there is anything going on between the two of them."

Del shrugged. "I don't really give a damn, but I want to make sure it doesn't give us any issues, since they didn't end well, from what all of us understand."

"Yeah, they seem to still be hands-off."

He nodded. "I have an interview with Harrington today."

"Former SEAL?"

"Yeah. I did a phone interview with him, and he's my pick out of the three possibilities. The other two have issues."

"And they live on the mainland."

"Yeah, that's one of the issues."

"What about Harrington?"

"Lived here the last three years, and he spent part of his childhood on the island."

That always made it easier. A lot of people moved to Hawaii thinking every day would be like a vacation. But if you wanted to earn a living, it wasn't. Same shit happened on Oahu that happened back on the mainland. He didn't really want to train with someone on their unit, then lose them when island fever hit them.

"Okay. Sounds good."

"I'll let you know how it goes." Del frowned. "Why are you here? You should be at home sleeping."

He would rather be doing that, but he couldn't seem to settle. *Ever.* Not these days. He didn't know what that said about him. "I have a few things to do, then I will. I didn't know the FBI had taken over the body from last night, or I would have stayed home. Why are you here?"

"Interview. Then I will go home."

"Okay. Text if you need me. I've got some paper-work." He bit back a groan as he stood. He was getting too old for all-nighters and then working the next day.

"You really need a life."

"I live vicariously through you," Adam said with a laugh. He hoped it didn't sound as stale as it felt. He shut the door and headed to his office. Adam had learned a long time ago that wishing for things ended in pain, especially when the one woman he wanted was unreachable.

Chapter Four

M arcus opened the door to the hotel room and held it for her. She stepped through the doorway and ignored his look. She wasn't in the mood for him or his idiotic ideas about their "relationship". Part of the problem had been him, and the other part had been her. But his issue was commitment, and he always thought the world revolved around him. She worried this would come up during their work, but until now, it hadn't been an issue. They had never worked a case before this, so there was a good chance it was just this. Or maybe it was just his dumbass way to pass time.

She pushed those thoughts aside and stood in the living area looking out the floor to ceiling windows. Golubev had to have dropped a fortune on the room. It wasn't high season, but rooms like this were several thousand a night.

The living area was completely pristine, other than the fingerprint powder. The staff wasn't allowed to come in, but she knew she and Marcus were on borrowed time.

"Something's off," Marcus said.

"Yeah." She walked around the suite trying to get the feel of the hit. She wasn't that good with murder, just as she had thought before. Strike that. She was good, but she didn't like dealing with it. Give her surveillance to go through and she was a happy camper. Murders were messy. She liked everything tied up in a neat little bow.

Marcus ducked into the bathroom.

"Anything?" she called out.

He shook his head as he stepped out into the living area again. "Charity probably has all the evidence."

She grimaced.

"What?"

"We're good, but I wonder now who called it in."

"The manager."

She nodded. Something odd slipped down her spine, something that chilled her soul. She didn't know what was leaving her so unsettled. Was it her conversation with Addie, or just the job? Or was it the man in the room with her? Nope, it was the hit.

"This feels like a setup."

He grunted. "Not sure it's that, but…if he was here with a woman, where is she? Wouldn't they kill her too?"

"That's a good point. He wouldn't come here for a woman, like to see a woman. To impress a woman...yeah."

"So, you don't think he came here to meet a woman?"

"Not in the sense that she was here, and he was pursuing her. That she wanted to come here, yes. Or that she said for sure she would let him bed her if he paid for her to be here."

"He sounds like an ass."

She chuckled. "He was from what I understand. I never met him."

"I have a feeling the FBI probably has stuff from his room that they didn't allow us to see."

She settled her hands on her hips. "More than likely."

Marcus walked into the bedroom. "Damn, glad we missed this."

Tamilya followed him through the door. The sheets had been stripped from the bed, but the blood had stained the mattress. "He or she used a silencer."

"Yeah. They found him last night because he'd arranged for room service to deliver at two a.m."

"Must be nice," she murmured.

"Alright, he was on the bed, or they moved him there?"

"He was on the bed. Had to be. If it's a hit..." she said, waiting for his nod. "Then we could very well be looking at a woman as the killer."

"Yeah."

She knelt on the floor and used her flashlight to look under the bed. It was clean, she knew that it would be. A woman, or a man masquerading as a woman, had lured him here, then shot him, execution style. She scanned the floor beneath the bed, and almost gave up until she saw a flash of white on the bed frame. "Hey, there's a scrap of paper over there on your side."

She kept the light on it until Marcus grabbed the paper. They both rose.

"Ala Moana."

"What?" she asked.

"Ala Moana. That's what it says."

"It was ripped from a bigger piece of paper. Hell, it could be from three weeks ago."

"Still, good catch," he said, slipping the paper into an evidence bag.

"Okay, so what now? Adam's contacts can't meet with us right now," she said just as both of their phones alerted them to texts.

"I guess we go back for the meeting. Elle has the results of the autopsy and, apparently, TJ made sure all the evidence was sent over to us. We were right," Marcus said. "They were holding things back, but he made sure we got it.

She smiled. "More like Charity made sure."

"That's true. Let's get going."

She nodded and looked around the room again.

"What?"

"Not sure. It's like something is missing."

"Maybe it's because most of the evidence was collected. Or, I should say all of the evidence was collected."

Her phone rang and she saw Charity's face. Their lab tech was one of the best in her field.

"Hey, woman," Charity said before Tamilya had a chance to say anything.

"Hey, yourself. Was there something you needed?"

"No. I just wanted to let you know that TJ brought by some more of the evidence."

"I saw that in the text."

"Oh, hmmm."

"What is it you really want to know?"

"So, you're working with Marcus on this case?"

She rolled her eyes. "Goodbye, Charity."

Tamilya clicked off her phone.

"What was that about?"

She shook her head and walked back out into the living area, then out the door. They were on the elevator before he said anything.

"Tammy," he said.

"I told you not to use that name anymore. It makes people think they can use it too."

He didn't say anything, so she glanced at him. He did not look happy with her. Tough kitties.

"Listen, I know that you have unresolved feelings or thoughts about our relationship. I don't. And while I don't want to belittle you for what you feel, I also don't want it spilling over into our work. Please, I need to keep this part of my life above board. I know you understand that."

He sighed and nodded, but said nothing else. A few people got on when the elevator stopped. Marcus might not like the situation, but it was one of his own doing. For her part, she wouldn't lose her focus.

Not for him or anyone else.

MARCUS WAS STILL IRRITATED when they got back to the office. He knew he had pushed it today, even though it hadn't been that much. When they walked into the common area, everyone but Adam and Del was sitting at the conference table.

"Hey," Charity said with a smile.

Everyone turned to look at them.

"What's going on?" Marcus asked.

"We're waiting on the boss. He's finishing up an interview," Autumn said. "And the guy is hot."

Marcus blinked. "Should you be saying things like that at work?"

"Sorry, but SEALS are hot, no matter what."

"He's a SEAL?" Tamilya asked.

Autumn nodded. "Adam told me before he left. And I

think we need to have a talk about Adam because he's been down lately."

Marcus frowned. "He seemed fine to me."

"Of course he did. You're a dude." Her gaze shifted back to the office. "Oh, they're coming out."

He rolled his eyes and glanced at Tamilya, whose face had lightened, and a smile curved her lips.

"Harry?"

He looked at the guy standing next to Del. Tall, at least six-five and all muscle. Of course he was. He was a SEAL, if Autumn was right. But it was the intimate way Tamilya said the guy's name that caught Marcus' attention.

"Tamilya? Hey," the guy—Harry—whatever, said.

He strode over to her and wrapped his arms around her lifting her off the floor. She squealed, which was completely un-Tamilya like.

"Put me down, you idiot," she said, but she was laughing.

"So, your lass knows the SEAL," Graeme said. Marcus glanced at the Scottish transplant and husband to their medical examiner, but he said nothing. He turned back to the bastard, who was about to lose his arms because he still had them around Tamilya.

"I take it you two know each other," Del said.

"Yeah," the SEAL said. "We go back a few years. I thought you were working with Dillon."

She shrugged. "You know I always liked working with the government."

"Why don't you introduce us to him, Tamilya?" Autumn said.

"Okay," she said with a smile. "Everyone, this is Seth Harrington, better known as Harry."

"To everyone except my mother."

"Why didn't I know you were on the island?"

"Work."

She nodded. "Coming over to the dark side?"

"That's up to your boss. I take it there's a staff meeting we're holding up?"

She nodded. "I'll walk you out, unless Del has anything else to talk to you about?"

"No, we were done," Del said.

"Thank you again for considering me," Harry said. "Nice to meet all of you."

Marcus watched as they walked out of the office, Harry's arm still wrapped around Tamilya's shoulders.

"Hmm, you don't know this dude?" Autumn asked.

"No. It's not like she knows all the women I dated."

Of course, none of them looked like they stepped off the cover of a volleyball calendar. With his blond hair and gray eyes, he could just imagine a lot of women went for those boy next door looks. The idea that Tamilya had dated Harrington was enough to make Marcus try to talk Del out of hiring him.

"Sure," Autumn said, but he didn't respond. He took one of the empty seats and handed Charity the evidence bag containing the slip of paper they'd found. "Not sure what it means, or if it had anything to do with Golubev, but Tamilya found this under the mattress on the bed frame."

———

"SO, YOU WORK FOR TFH?" Harry said as they walked side-by-side down the sidewalk.

"Yeah."

"I thought you had a good gig with Dillon."

"I did, but I got bored."

He chuckled. "You were never meant to take orders from rich people. That's a lot of what you did, wasn't it?"

She nodded. "I did workups for a lot of companies who had to worry about terrorism."

"Defense contractors?"

"In a way. You know the way of the military industrial complex now."

"And personal security," he said.

"Yeah. *That* I did not like."

"I can imagine. You like TFH?"

She nodded. "I do. Del's a good boss and the number two, Adam Lee, is fantastic."

"Cool."

The silence stretched out comfortably. There had never been any tension in their relationship outside of the bedroom. "I didn't know you were getting out. You didn't mention it when we last talked."

"That was over a year ago."

She sensed something had happened that he did not want to talk about.

"I didn't know that you would be able to work with Floyd again."

Tamilya had met Harry not long after she had left the FBI and still had a chip on her shoulder. That and a broken heart. He was probably the only one who knew how badly Marcus had hurt her. They had dated more out of solace than anything else. Harry's marriage had died a slow death thanks to an unfaithful wife and a bastard friend.

Their relationship had never been about romance but

more about comfort. They both needed to heal with a nonjudgmental partner. She'd been in DC working for Dillon Security on a job out of the Miami office when they'd met. They had a brief affair, and then they went their separate ways as friends.

"It was more the team. They're family. Or Ohana."

"I got a little of that talking with Del."

She nodded.

"We need to do dinner," he said.

"After this case I'm working on. I have a feeling we'll have it wrapped up soon, but I want to make sure."

He nodded and leaned closer to brush his lips over her cheek. "Give me a call when you get done."

She nodded. "Will do."

She watched him walk to his car. The rush of feelings, the need to connect with him that had been so present a few years ago, wasn't there. The friendship was still strong, but the desire to connect on a more intimate level wasn't.

With a sigh, she headed back into the building. She wished she did have those feelings. He was stable, easygoing, and always supportive of her. Her life would be easier if she could be with a man like Harry. As she stepped into the office, everyone turned in mass once again. She chuckled to herself. Definitely like a family.

Then she caught sight of Marcus, who was frowning at her. And just like that, her pulse quickened. A flush of heat swept over her body. A need she didn't understand left her breathless. She really *was* an idiot. This man was bad for her. They were bad together.

"So, are we ready?" Elle, their medical examiner, asked.

Tamilya nodded as she took her seat next to Marcus.

"Our Russian died thanks to the bullet wound to the back of his head. Not very distinguishable in the world of hired killers, I know. But he was beaten up before the murder."

"Beaten up?" Marcus asked.

Elle nodded. "He had three broken ribs that hadn't started to heal; therefore, I'm assuming they happened right around the same time." She clicked on her tablet and the screen showed Golubev, post autopsy. His torso and face were covered with purple and yellow bruises. "These were not present this morning. They appeared while I was performing the autopsy, which tells me they happened in the hour leading up to his death."

"So someone beat him up then killed him," Tamilya said. "I'm assuming they wanted something from him."

"Not money," Charity said. She took over the tablet, tapping her fingers over the screen. "He has little of that. Most of it had been drained out. It took me awhile, and many threats to my husband, but we now know that Golubev was using the name Allen Smith."

Marcus snorted. "Are you kidding me?"

Charity rolled her eyes. "Right? Could they get any more generic?"

"And he had a thick Russian accent, unless he got rid of it," Tamilya said.

"I thought you didn't know much about him," Marcus said.

"I don't, but Addie said it was one of the things she would always remember about him. He was lazy, so I doubt he tried to get rid of it."

"That definitely would have alerted people," Charity said. "Anyway, he had been spending large amounts of money. Dinners, hotel rooms, flowers."

"A woman," Tamilya said.

Charity nodded. "Yeah, that's what TJ heard from his handler."

"They were just letting him run around unsupervised?" Graeme asked.

"Looks like it. And boyfriend had some expensive tastes. I know a few of these restaurants from my time in DC and Marcel's is pricey. And it was consistently dinner for two."

Tamilya nodded in agreement. "He was in lust with someone and spending a lot of money."

"I've asked for the surveillance in and around these areas. I should be able to find out what was going on and with whom soon enough."

"Good," Del said. "Anything on the bullet?"

"Nope. I am casting a wider net, and I hope to have something later today," Charity said.

Del turned to Marcus and Tamilya. "Do you two think that there are any national security concerns here? I have to brief the mayor and governor this afternoon, and I want to make sure we let them know."

"Right now, I can't say. If we can get an image of whoever he was romancing, then we might know. I doubt she has anything to do with the murder."

"Why do you say that?" Del asked.

"He usually went for stupid women. Or those who appeared to be stupid. They were always flashy, over the top. He was a man who liked to pretend he had connections, but he really didn't."

"Then why was the FBI using him?"

"He might not have the connections, but he did play in those circles, socially speaking. I think he could have become very powerful in Russia. Money is power, and he was very good at kissing ass from what I read about him. But, while he would fund some terrorism, he wanted enough to live in luxury. He didn't understand working hard at all."

Del nodded. "And you're going to talk to some of Adam's contacts?"

"Yeah, just got a message from one of them that he could meet with us this afternoon," Marcus said.

"Good. Anything else?" Everyone shook their heads. "Okay. Go work, catch bad guys, all that crap. Tamilya, could I talk to you for a minute?"

She nodded. "What time did you say we would meet his contact?" she asked Marcus.

"We have another hour, so plenty of time."

She followed Del into his office. "Shut the door, would you?"

She nodded and shut the door. He sat behind his desk, and she took one of the two chairs in front of his desk.

"How long have you known Harry?"

"A few years."

"I take it you were involved with him."

She nodded.

"Can you give me an idea of what he's like?"

"Hard worker, job always came first with him. Committed to doing the right thing. I used to call him Captain America because of his need to always put others first."

"But?"

"What?"

"You have some worries about him."

She shook her head. "I'm just wondering where he fits into a team like TFH."

"Ah, okay. I haven't told the team, but the governor

wants us to fill out the team some more. They want divisions."

"Divisions?"

"Yeah, or I should say maybe smaller teams. They definitely want us to start off with a Search and Rescue group. We would all still work together. I do need someone to lead training and be the POC for the HPD, but where we do training for investigative work, they would concentrate more on new search and rescue techniques."

"And you want Harry to help with that?" He nodded. "Well, he would be excellent. I know that it was one of his favorite parts of the job."

"Anything else?"

"Well, he is a bit of a workaholic, then again, that's pretty much the team."

He smiled. "True."

"You need to go home, boss."

"I will after I do this briefing with the mayor and governor. I plan on sleeping for a day."

"Anything else?"

He shook his head.

"You don't want to ask about my relationship with Harry?"

"No. That's your personal business. Just keep any issues out of work."

People said things like that, but she never knew anyone who really believed that but Del. It was one of the things she liked most about working for him. "No problem."

"Let me know what you and Floyd find out."

"Will do."

She stepped out of the office and a hush fell over the group at the table. Marcus wasn't around.

"Where did Marcus go?" she asked.

"He went with Charity to log in that evidence. He said he'd be back in a second," Autumn said. "Do you think we'll be able to do dinner tonight still?"

She and Autumn were the newest members and had struck up a kind of relationship. They would get together for dinner or drinks, every now and then.

"I don't see why not. I'll let you know if something takes off."

"Cool. Just let me know."

"I'll text you. I have a feeling this was just a man being stupid. I looked over the evidence list. There was not one item of his found other than his clothes. Money was gone but credit cards remained."

Autumn nodded. "Yeah, I was thinking there should be some bling, right?"

"Definitely. He would have very little money in the bank but a Rolex that cost more than all of my college tuition on his wrist."

"I saw a pic from an FBI report. He had a lot of chains on."

Tamilya nodded.

"So, want to tell me about this Harry dude?"

She shrugged. "We dated awhile when I was living in DC."

"After Marcus?"

"Yeah."

"No feelings?"

Tamilya blinked. "No. We're still really good friends but that's it."

"First, please don't tell Marcus that because I want to see him get all hot and bothered by it."

"He didn't..." her voice trailed off when Autumn

crossed her arms beneath her breasts and nodded. "Oh, well, no reason to. Our split was mutual, and we've remained friends."

"Also, you don't mind if I hit that, do you?"

Anger surged. "Marcus?" she asked, trying to keep her voice as neutral as possible.

"Oh, man," Autumn said chuckling. "You're pissed about that."

"Am not."

"That was mature, but I will let it go. No. The SEAL."

"Oh. Sure. He's a really good guy. And don't talk like you're some kind of player."

In fact, Autumn was a virgin at the ripe age of thirty. It was hard to trust people after being raised in a cult, but she had only told Tamilya about her virginity. While she might seem open, Autumn was a very private person about some things. Her sex life was one of them.

"Oh, there's Marcus," she said with a smile. She leaned closer before Tamilya could look over at him. "He's gonna want to talk to you about the SEAL. Tell him you're going to have dinner with him."

"Stop that," she said. "Ready?" she asked Marcus when he stepped up to them.

He nodded, but didn't say anything. So this was going to be fun.

"Text me," Autumn said, heading off to her office.

As she and Marcus walked out of the office, the tension seemed to grow with each step. In the past, Tamilya could ignore things like this. An African-American woman didn't rise in the ranks of the FBI without that ability. There was always someone who thought she didn't belong.

But with Marcus, it was different. It always was.

"Go ahead," she said.

He glanced at her before he slipped on his mirrored sunglasses. "What?"

"I know you want to ask about Harry."

"Actually, I do have a question."

They stepped outside and she frowned. It wasn't the bright sun she was used to. Instead, clouds were rolling in signaling that the light showers would soon arrive.

"Okay."

"When did you and Bradford start hanging out?"

She opened her mouth to deny him an answer when she realized he'd asked about Autumn.

"A couple of months ago."

He grunted as he continued on, not looking at her.

"That's it? A grunt?"

He shrugged. "You seem like an odd match up as friends."

"What's that supposed to mean?"

He stopped in front of his SUV. "She's the quirky daughter of a cult leader. You're the by the book former FBI agent. Just odd."

He pressed his key fob to unlock his vehicle, then walked to the driver's door.

She followed suit, climbing up on her side.

"It's not really that odd," she said as he put the car in drive.

"Yeah, it is. Or rather, she is."

"Quirky." She corrected. "And she's actually pretty interesting."

"Why do you say that?"

"Really? She is one of a handful of survivors from the Joyous Wave Cult. Her father made David Koresh look normal. And yeah, at first, that's what intrigued me. Plus, we were the last two hired, so we're still trying to find our places on the team."

He nodded as he turned onto Ala Moana Avenue. "But you became friends."

"Yeah. We have some of the same taste in movies—not all women hate romantic comedies and love action adventure. My parents treat her like she's one of the family, which is kind of nice."

"I have yet to meet your parents. And I didn't even while we were dating."

He did *not* just go there. Of course he did. He was Marcus and that was the crap Marcus pulled sometimes. For months after their breakup, the one he initiated, he acted like the hurt party. There was always a part of her who thought he expected her to beg him to come back. There was one thing Tamilya did not do…and that was beg.

"I've been friends longer with Autumn than you and I were lovers."

"Damn, that's cold," he said with a chuckle.

"It's the truth. Also, she's kind of fragile."

He cut a look from the side of his eye. "Autumn?"

"Yeah, she doesn't show it, but she has no one in the world. No family. And I think my parents kind of sensed that."

"I hadn't thought of it that way. Both her parents died during the fighting, right?"

"Yeah. So Mom and Dad have treated her like one of their own."

He nodded. Changing the subject, he said, "The guy Adam suggested, that first one on the list, says he'll talk to us. He's the one who used to be in tight with arms dealers."

"Sounds good."

Keeping her mind focused on the investigation was most important. There was no need to rehash a relationship that was dead and long buried.

Chapter Five

Marcus and Tamilya walked side-by-side up to the door of a small house in the Salt Lake area. He'd looked at a few houses in this area when he first moved to Oahu, but he'd wanted to be connected to the bustle of Honolulu. Plus, depending on where your house was located in Salt Lake, you rarely got a good view. The traffic was horrific also. He liked that he could be at work in less than ten minutes.

It sat close to several of the bases and was definitely an easier commute to Honolulu than anywhere on the West End. Still, it wasn't something he wanted for himself. As they approached the little green house, the scent of plumeria hit him. No matter where he lived in the world after this, he would always associate the smell with his time in Hawaii.

He glanced at his companion and inwardly sighed. He never thought they would cross paths again until he'd found out she'd transferred to Hawaii herself. The first time they came face-to-face, he had understood what a dumbass he had been. Giving her up had been so damned stupid and cowardly.

Now, he was stuck in the friend zone. There just didn't seem to be any way to get through to her. Doing it on the job was off limits. While he didn't mind dating women he worked with, the strict line between work and personal needed to be definitive. No woman should have to deal with that on the job, especially when their lives were on the line.

From the first time he had seen her, he had wanted her. It had never happened like that for him before. Attraction was one thing. His need to have her almost overwhelmed his better judgement. He'd had a lot of affairs over his life, but none of them had been so combustible. It had been some kind of primal connection. Over these last few months, he'd come to know her even better. Tough as nails, with a soft center. She didn't put up with anyone's shit, but she could also show compassion. The story about Autumn was a prime example.

"You think this guy can help?" she asked.

Marcus had made a few contacts since he moved to Hawaii, but it was proving to be tougher than he'd thought it would be. Hawaii was a state, but it was also different than any state he had been in. They were a bit on their own out in the Pacific, and since they were the most geologically isolated place on the planet, they tended to be distrustful of outsiders. Not that he blamed them. Every time Hawaiians trusted another country, they ended up getting shafted.

"Maybe. He does have a good number of contacts within that world. He doesn't work with them anymore, but he has family."

"And we're going to trust him?"

Marcus shrugged. "Not like we have much choice. You know how this is. I also trust Adam."

"Right."

He hated that this guy wasn't his informant. Marcus didn't know him and while he trusted Adam, it didn't mean that either of them had to trust this guy. Or that he would be that truthful with them. Marcus just didn't like depending on other people's leads, and he knew Tamilya was the same way. That was what had left her out to dry in the Virginia Star Mall bombing.

Marcus leaned on the doorbell and they waited. A commotion of voices, several of them being children, erupted. A short, portly Asian man opened the door. He was wearing a Hawaiian shirt and board shorts. "Floyd?"

Marcus nodded. "Dennis?"

The man nodded as he looked between the two of them. "This is my associate Tamilya Lowe."

Adam must have given both of their names to Dennis because he nodded. "Francie, I have to talk to some people."

"Okay, babe," a woman called out.

Then he stepped out on the stoop and shut the door behind him. "I try to keep my family out of this and normally, I'd have you come in, but my youngest made the honor roll, so we're doing a cookout. Come on around to the back."

They followed him as he walked, barefooted, to the back of the house. There, a large grill was set up. He walked over and started the fire.

"Adam told me you want to know who to look for in a murder?"

"Yeah. He's a Russian, Golubev. Do you know of any hitmen Russians would hire?"

"I heard of him. Not much mind you, because my area was usually in Eastern Asia. There are a few possibilities I'll text you."

"You've heard of him," Tamilya said. "How?"

"There's been a few rumors about him for years, but I always thought he was kind of a blowhard."

"Something tells you he wasn't?"

"Not really. I still think he's an asshole, but I recently heard he put out a buy for some C4."

"Just openly asking for it?" Marcus asked.

The guy shrugged. "I understood he wasn't too smart. That's how he got pinged by the FBI I think."

"But that wasn't here, was it?" Tamilya asked.

He shook his head. "That was on the mainland. Virginia."

"Virginia?" she asked, a hitch in her voice.

"Yeah. There were always rumors that he had something to do with that mall bombing."

Ice sunk into his bones. He looked at Tamilya. She blinked and then glanced at Marcus. The questions in her gaze were filling his head. They both turned back to Dennis.

"Virginia Star Mall?" Marcus asked.

"Yeah, although I heard that he didn't have anything to do with that."

"Okay. But nothing lately?"

"Just that bit about the C-4, but most people thought he was involved at the time. When he was alive, he hung out with Dave Li."

"Li?" Marcus asked.

"I know of him," Tamilya said. "He's got ties to the Chinese government."

"Yeah. Him. And he's on the island, but I don't know

what he's doing here. Could be he's just got a little business. I don't ask too many questions because the guy is seriously insane."

"Business?" Marcus asked.

"He's a trafficker. Mainly for labor."

"Lovely," Tamilya said, sarcasm dripping from the word.

"Hey, don't look at me. I dealt arms, that's it. I walked away when I met Francie."

She nodded. "So, he knew this Li?"

"Yeah. And from what I know, Li has been known to do favors for the Chinese government. I mean more than usual."

"Favors?" Tamilya asked.

"Yeah. Targets in Taiwan, things like that. When they don't want it to tie back to them, they hire contractors. He's one of their favs."

Whatever was going on, it could be an issue for them. And if the Chinese were involved, it made more sense. Hawaii was a prize in the middle of the Pacific. PACCOM—the Indo-Pacific Command Forces at Camp Smith—was going to have a field day with this. If Golubev's murder was more than just a hit for money, they were going to be royally screwed.

"Anything else you can tell us?" Marcus asked.

"Not really. I told Adam I'll ask around. I still have family in the business, and they aren't going to be happy with some of this landing on their doorsteps."

"Mahalo," Marcus said, then he looked at Tamilya. "Anything else?"

She shook her head. "This gives us a little bit of info. Again, as Marcus said, let us know if you hear anything else."

"No problem, sista."

They didn't talk as they walked back to the vehicle. Marcus didn't know what it all meant. Golubev seemed to be a regular idiot, too much money, and the kind of mouth that ended up getting him killed. Marcus hoped that was all there was to it.

They were halfway back to the office when Tamilya finally said something. "There's something there that's bothering me."

"What?"

"First, the mention of Virginia Star Mall bombing. That's odd."

He nodded. "I agree with that," he said as they ground to a halt thanks to traffic.

Friday afternoon was a crap time to make a trip back into Honolulu, or anywhere else on the island for that matter. People on the mainland said Happy Aloha Friday, and Hawaiians lived it.

"What does his death have to do with any of this?" Tamilya asked out loud. It wasn't a question for him, he knew that. He'd worked with her in the past, and he knew the way she processed information. She brooded for a bit.

She pulled out her phone and began scrolling.

"What are you thinking?"

"I'm looking for the background on Golubev. There was something on there about civilian targets."

He sighed with relief when the traffic started moving again, giving him enough room to take the Pali Highway exit.

"Yeah, here it is. His parents died in a terrorist attack, by a Chechen. He supports terrorist attacks against federal and state facilities but will not help anyone who wants to attack civilians."

"Then linking his name to the Virginia Star Mall bombing makes no sense. That targeted civilians."

She grunted and it made Marcus smile. He knew that most people would look at a woman like Tamilya with her fine bone structure and beauty and think she would never do anything like grunt when irritated.

"It was a fine line. Adrien Popov left notes that said he picked it because the large number of military families that used the mall. It was the closest mall to Belvoir."

"True," he said, turning onto the street that led to their headquarters. Popov had been considered the planner and sole perpetrator. "I'll do a little hunting around for connections between the two of them."

"Okay. Let me get hold of Autumn and call off our night out together."

"Nah, let me take care of it. First, I think this is just a scam."

"A scam?"

"Yeah. Sure, he was here, but he wouldn't show up where he's going to do a job. He's not the type to get his hands dirty. He's the kind that would hire people and then sit back and enjoy the pain he inflicted."

"You're right. Damn."

"No, it might mean we are off the hook. If there is no terrorism involved, maybe he was just stupid enough to get himself caught in some kind of scam. He's the kind of guy who would get catfished."

She snorted. "True. So, I'm still going to do my dinner, but if something comes up, I want you to text me. I don't want to shirk my duties."

He pulled to a stop at a light. "No worries, Tammy. Go out and have fun. Hopefully, I can put this to bed tonight. If it is an old-fashioned murder case, we'll be done with it in no time. In fact, we can lob it back to the FBI to handle."

She offered him a smile, and he felt like he'd won the lottery. For a smile. Not a grin or a laugh. But a freaking smile that she probably offered other people, but rarely gave him one. Not these days, at least. He realized that he was gripping the steering wheel so hard his knuckles ached. He used to be a player. He'd have women lined up begging for a date. Then…it changed.

Tamilya. They were sitting at a light and he glanced over at her. She noticed and looked up.

"What?"

"Nothing."

She nodded. "It's green."

"What?"

"The light," she said just as someone behind them laid on their horn.

He shook his head and hit the gas.

"Maybe I should take care of this and you go home," she said amused.

"Naw," he said.

What had changed? That would be the woman sitting next to him right now. Their short, intense affair had scared the crap out of him. He hadn't admitted it then, but he constantly reminded himself these days. Every time they'd made love, he'd felt those ties growing tighter, and, in the end, he had told himself he didn't need that kind of distraction.

He had never been so wrong in his life.

He parked his SUV but didn't move to get out. He had wanted this for months, but most of their interactions were during meetings. Now, he had encouraged her to go out with Autumn, which probably would be at some damned bar filled with tourists looking for a good time.

Fuck.

"Did you say something?" she asked.

Marcus glanced at her and shook his head.

"Okay."

She said nothing else. After she slipped out of the SUV, he drew in a deep breath and ordered himself under control. When he thought he might be able to act like an adult and not some angsty teen, he followed her out of the SUV. She was on the phone.

"We're back. What's up?" she asked. She listened for a long time.

"Why can't you just tell me?"

Another session of listening stretched out as Tamilya's expression turned darker. Who the hell was on the other end of the line?

"Fine, we can come down."

Well, he had his answer. Charity would be the only one who worked downstairs who would have anything for them. Tamilya clicked her phone off and looked at Marcus, but she didn't truly see him. Her gaze was unfocused. She was nibbling on her lower lip, deep in thought, and there was no doubt something was bothering her.

"Was that Charity?" he asked, wanting to confirm his suspicions.

She nodded. "She said she had some info on the ballistics. She wants us down there right now."

"Why couldn't she just tell you over the phone?"

"Right?" she asked as she started walking for the front door to TFH. "That's the thing that's bothering me."

Her frown darkened as they stepped into headquarters and walked to the elevators. He didn't know what to say to lighten her load. He wasn't a guy who thought women should always be happy and smiling, but whenever he thought she might be hurting, suffering, he wanted to fix it.

When the elevator doors opened, they stepped off the car. Charity was already calling them.

"She's loud, and that's from a woman who has two sisters."

"Yeah, I know your pain."

For a second, they shared a smile and he felt a little bit better. He knew this case might cause her undo worries. Virginia Star was in the past, but having it slip into their investigation, even if it led nowhere, couldn't be easy to deal with.

When they stepped into the forensics lab, he saw TJ.

"Hey," he said with a strained smile. "Did you guys get anything good?"

He shook his head. "Only that Golubev was linked to Li."

"Ah, damn."

"That was my feeling on the subject," Tamilya said. "Just what this mess needs is to be tangled up with the Chinese."

He nodded. "That brings a lot of other implications into the investigation. We are already having issues with China, but this would blow that up."

"Hopefully he was just killed as some kind of scam," Marcus said, trying to cheer them all up. Hell, he was trying to cheer himself up.

"Sorry," Charity said shaking her head. She shared a glance with her husband, then her gaze settled on Tamilya. "But it isn't going to be that easy."

"What?" Tamilya asked, and he heard the tension in her voice.

"We linked the bullet in Golubev's brain."

Tamilya looked at Marcus, then she looked back to Charity. "Tell us."

Sympathy and regret stamped Charity's expression. "The gun was used in the Virginia Star bombing."

Chapter Six

For a long few moments, Tamilya stood still, unable to think…to even breathe. *This can't be happening.*

Spots formed in front her eyes as she tried to deal with the waves of hysteria that threatened to take over. She tried to swallow and found it impossible. She felt a hand at her back. Strong, warm, dependable. Marcus.

"Breathe," he said softly.

He was the calm in the storm that was threatening to drown her. Corny, but it fit. Because of his support, she drew in a deep breath and released it slowly. Tamilya's heartbeat slowed down and there were no longer any spots in front of her eyes.

"Thanks," she murmured.

"Anytime, Tammy." he said.

She didn't object to his use of the nickname, couldn't. His voice rolled over the syllables, and while many times she found it sexy, right now, she found it comforting. The fact that she wanted to curl herself up into his embrace and ignore this was enough to scare her. She had learned long ago that Marcus didn't like ties beyond the bedroom.

Drawing in a deep breath, she released it slowly and straightened her shoulders.

"So, tell us about this bullet," she said.

"It's from the gun used in the killing of the security guard at the mall."

"Damn," Marcus said. "Are you sure?"

Charity gave him an irritated look. "Of course I am."

"This shines a light on what one of our CIs told us today. He was linking Golubev to the bombing."

"I still disagree with that," Tamilya said.

"Why?" TJ asked her. He wasn't challenging her. He was just *that* interested in their theories.

"I looked him up, and he had a thing about bombing or harming civilians. It's how he lost his parents, so he refused to work with anyone targeting that sector."

"But, like you said, there were a high number of military families who were there. Most of the casualties were from military personnel and their families," Marcus said,

She fought back the need to correct him. Not because she thought he was right, but she knew she had a knee jerk reaction to anything related to that particular bombing. Why would he have anything to do with that? He never had any big links to terrorism in the US. He mainly went after Chechen rebels.

"When did the FBI fake his death?" Tamilya asked.

"What?" TJ asked.

She looked at Marcus. The moment she did, she knew the two of them were on the same page. She could see it there in his expression. She tore her attention away from Marcus and looked at TJ. "When did he come to the FBI?"

He blinked, then she saw the recognition in his eyes.

"Let me look it up, but it wasn't too long after the bombing."

TJ pulled out his phone and started working on the answer.

"What are you getting at?" Charity said.

"What if he was involved in the bombing, but he thought it was going to be military targets?"

"Oh…oh! Yeah. That would piss him off if he didn't want civilian deaths," Charity said.

"Our CI told us there were rumors that he was linked to Li. He has connections to several hits mainly where China has interests. Hitting the US would be different for him."

"And, let's be honest, the Chinese wouldn't want people to know they were linked," Marcus said.

"Why not?" Charity asked.

"First, they would like the idea of screwing with us. Causing our morale to plummet," Marcus said.

"Yeah. Just like the Russians messing with our social media, there has always been forces in the Chinese government that wanted to do the same thing."

Tamilya's phone buzzed and she recognized the number. Addie.

"Give me a second," she said as she stepped away and then clicked on her phone. "Hey, Addie, what's up."

"I was wondering if you've had any other developments in the case?"

Tamilya hesitated for a second before answering. She didn't like the fact that her old boss seemed to call right at the very moment that they all figured out this might be connected to Virginia Star.

"Not at this time. Just a few leads and that Golubev might be linked to Li."

Addie made a rude noise, and Tamilya knew at once that she wasn't pleased with the situation. She honestly didn't blame her old boss. When you are about to walk out the door with your pension and a great new job waiting for you, having the biggest screw up in your career popping back up isn't the best occurrence. It was actually the worst. If the FBI decided to reinvestigate the case, it could put her retirement on hold, and she could very well lose the job she had lined up.

"Right now I am taking it all with a grain of salt."

Tamilya was lying, she just hoped that Addie didn't catch on. Her old boss was sharp, but being on the phone these many miles apart, Tamilya hoped she didn't get caught. They didn't need Addie sticking her nose into their business.

"Yes, well, you will keep me up to date, right?"

She asked it as if it were a question, but Tamilya heard it more as a warning. Addie might have been treating Tamilya as her protégé, but she knew the agent hadn't thought twice when Tamilya's job came under fire. She'd tossed her to the side the moment Tamilya became a liability.

"I will, especially if I get a bead on anything you can help with."

A beat of silence. "Thanks. I don't have many days left, but I would rather not go out with a whimper," she said with a laugh.

"No problem, Addie. I'll let you know."

"Thanks," she said, and Tamilya hung up without saying anything else.

There was definitely something bothering Tamilya about Addie, but she couldn't put her finger on it. Was she afraid that this case coming up would screw her chances at her new job? Hell, if anything came out now, she could lose her retirement. With the daggers out for law enforcement, nothing was sacred. One mistake could ruin your entire career. Since Addie was the most opportunistic woman Tamilya had ever met—and that said a lot since she'd been to high school with not one, but three Miss USA state champions—that had to be the reason.

She walked back over to Charity, TJ, and Marcus. All of them looked at her, but it was Marcus' attention that disturbed her the most. The longer he looked at her, the more she felt her body temperature rise. When she realized she was ignoring the other two people in the room, she tore her attention away from him.

"I've called the boss," Charity said. "He wants a meeting in thirty. Everyone is coming back in."

Autumn came around the corner from the direction of her office. "Except for me, because I'm here. I'm assuming that our night out is off?" she asked with a twitch of her lips.

"Yeah," Tamilya said with sigh. "I think we need other jobs."

"Oh, do you know of some other job that will allow us to carry guns and shoot people?"

Tamilya snorted, her shoulder muscles relaxing just a bit. Autumn was an odd duck, but she always seemed to understand what Tamilya needed to help her chill out.

"The boss wants you to give a rundown of the Virginia Star Mall incident. I'm going to gather up the figures and make the slides, but I know he wants you to let us know what the official word was and what you think happened," Charity said.

"What do you mean?" Tamilya asked.

"We all know that you're a kick ass agent; so I, for one,

want to know what the FBI got wrong," she said, glancing at her husband.

TJ held his hands up. "Hey, I wasn't part of that, and I agree with you." He looked at Tamilya. "You're too sharp not to have picked up on a few issues out of the norm."

She felt the backs of her eyes start to burn, and she blinked away the tears that threatened to fall. These people who had known her for such a short amount of time compared to her FBI colleagues didn't question her thought process. Then, there was Marcus.

They were never going to be a couple again, but the fact that she knew he had her back, meant the world to her. It was giving her all those warm, fuzzy feelings she'd mistook for love previously. She pushed them aside. She could take his admiration and work with him. That was all she wanted or needed from Marcus.

"I'll help you with those slides," she said as Charity turned to leave. She hurried to catch up before Charity made it to the elevator doors. As soon as the doors slid closed, she drew in a deep breath.

"Girl, that man has a hankering for you."

Tamilya hated the way the words made her heart jump. She didn't need him, or the heartache he would definitely give her. If it had been bad before, it would be ten times worse this time around. And if she reminded herself every five minutes, she just might remember that.

MARCUS HATED that he had to watch Tamilya give a briefing. No, strike that. He liked it, he just hated sharing her with everyone else. He wanted her all to himself and everyone else could go get bent.

Charity was just about finished going through the timeline of the Virginia Star bombing, and he knew Tamilya would take over. Tammy. God, he loved using that name for her. It was intimate. He could just imagine saying it against her flesh as he kissed his way over her stomach.

"Lowe, you're up," Del said, breaking into Marcus' fantasy.

Damn, he hadn't been paying any attention, but he knew all the facts about the Virginia Star bombing. He'd been in DC at the time. Still, thinking about tasting Tamilya left him half erect like he was a teenager without the ability to control himself. He shifted in his chair trying to ease the pressure in his pants. The chair squeaked loudly in the silence and everyone turned to look at him. Damn.

Tamilya ignored him and stepped up.

"So, what we had was three dead terrorists, and numerous dead civilians. We were still going over the data, getting the bodies examined, when they claimed all the bombers had died in the incident. There were a few issues with this," she said, her voice true and strong.

She clicked on her iPad and the pictures of several different people appeared. "We had four dead people who had been wounded before the explosion, and one that had been killed."

"Wait, what?" Elle asked. "I read the report. That wasn't in there."

Tamilya nodded. "That's why I threw a fit when they announced that all the bombers were dead. Not one of those guys had ever shown up on any watchlist. They'd never even shown a propensity for violence or hatred toward the US. Don't get me wrong, they could have had those feelings, but because the FBI was worried about PR at the time, they wanted simple answers."

"You didn't think they did it?" Del asked.

"I think they did. I didn't know their reasons though. When someone is a terrorist, why they choose that path is as important as what they did. We need to know why they wanted to participate. If they acted of their own free will, then where did they go wrong? What had pushed them over the edge?"

"Why is that important?" Autumn asked.

"If we know where they got recruited, we can start looking for more. It's like IEDs in Afghanistan and Iraq. As soon as the military comes up with a way to detect one, they have ten more ways to build and activate them. So, if we could figure it out, it would help us at least stop the recruitment there."

"You said 'if they acted of their own free will.' What do you mean?" Del asked.

"They could have been blackmailed or forced to participate in some other way. There were rumors about Pavlov being gay, which was a dangerous thing to be if you're Russian. The other two had some massive debt, but all of them had family members in Russia. We know that many people would get stuck in Soviet Russia due to not wanting to leave their families. That practice has not changed today."

"So, these five people, who were they and where do they fit in the big scheme of things?" Del asked.

She clicked on her iPad and the five people's pics came up. "All of them worked in some capacity at the Mall. Grissom here," she said highlighting an older looking white man, "was the security guard. We had video of someone shooting him, then the feeds went dead, so we assumed that was planned. The others seemed to make no sense, unless it was just wrong place wrong time kind of thing."

She brought up the other people again. "Fiona Marshall worked in the operations office for the Mall. Sort of a secretarial kind of job. Cassie Bigelow, Sam Johnson, and Dylan Busch worked at various stores, but they were all on their breaks at the time, from what we could tell. There was a little area for Mall employees to go eat. The smaller store employees tended to go there, as the big department stores had their own break rooms."

"They weren't all found in the same area though," Charity said.

"Exactly. My thoughts were that their passes were used to help the bombers get into areas that are off-limits to regular people. Virginia Star was a different kind of mall in that respect. They had a lot of underground areas, which required an employee pass."

"Why didn't they just steal one? Wouldn't that have been easier?" Cat asked.

Tamilya shrugged. "I do know the mall was extremely particular about those passes. They had a monthly check to make sure people had theirs. All shops had to maintain a list and, if not, each missing badge incurred a five hundred dollar fine."

Del whistled. "Damn, that's expensive."

She nodded. "So, it made sense that they watched schedules and then singled out four people they could easily grab. Fiona, we think just walked in on the situation and they shot her. She was found right outside of the break room. Each of the others were found in a location where the bombs were detonated."

"Why did the FBI hide this?" Charity said crossing her arms beneath her chest, glaring at TJ.

"Hey, I didn't have anything to do with it."

"And, as Elle pointed out, it was hidden from the public as well. Which I thought was stupid. I didn't realize it though until months later."

After she had left the FBI, Marcus thought. She was never going to let it go and now it exploded in her face. Granted, she looked composed and fine with the situation, but he knew Tamilya well, and she was *not* composed. She was a bundle of nerves.

"Did you ever call Addie on it?" he asked.

She nodded. "Addie was my old supervisor. She said that by the time they were able to find the last of the bodies, they realized the mistake. On top of that, she used some lame excuse that they were trying to spare the families any more grief."

"More like they were trying to cover up that they didn't have all the answers," Marcus said.

She nodded. "As I said earlier, I always had problems with events as they were reported. I knew at first they were holding information back, as we do with any active investigation."

"But something changed?" Charity asked.

Marcus watched TJ and Tamilya share a look. They had both been in the FBI at the time, and TJ had a mentor kind of relationship with her. Still, he couldn't fight the jealousy snaking through his system. He balled his fist against his thigh beneath the table so no one could see. It made no sense that he was feeling this way. TJ was seriously happy in his marriage to Charity, and there had never been any evidence that TJ and Tamilya were even interested in each other. Still, he wanted to punch TJ in the face—at least twice.

"Yeah. The blame game started very early on. I'll never know who started the rumors, the ones that said our team—especially me—was sabotaging the investigation. That we—again, me in particular—were trying to make a name for ourselves."

"That makes no bloody sense," Graeme said, piping up for the first time. "You would never do something like that."

There were a few more grunts around the table that he knew were agreeing with Graeme's comments.

Tamilya's features softened and Marcus realized she had worried about the team. And why wouldn't she? She had been stabbed in the back by those closest to her at the FBI.

"Thank you for that. Their reasoning was that we invented a wider conspiracy to cover for the fact that we missed the signs."

"But you were the one who found them," TJ said frowning. "I understand some FBI bullshit, but that part of the Virginia Star bombing never made sense. You found the first signs that Northern Virginia was the focus of a hit."

"Exactly, but you know what the management of the FBI is like. They are all political, and they have no problem throwing anyone—including a loved one—under the bus."

"And then there was Addie," Marcus said, trying his best not to spit out her name.

Tamilya shook her head. "She had nothing to do with it and more to lose than having her protégé go under like I did. Granted, she didn't protect me, so I don't completely trust her."

"You think she had something to do with the bombing?" Del asked.

"God, no. Just that she's a creature who puts herself first, and everything she sees is viewed through that very self-serving lens. Even with her leaving the bureau, she will want to make sure this makes her look good."

Marcus had to agree.

"Do you think sharing information with her is a problem?" Cat asked.

Everyone looked at TJ.

"Oh, hey, I'm not listening to any of this."

Tamilya sighed. "I want to keep her in the dark about some things. Mainly because she never understood discretion within the FBI. You never tell everyone everything. There's a reason for the different security levels."

"Okay. I won't tell her anything you don't clear for me to tell her. Of course, I will deny it if the FBI asks," TJ said with a smile.

She nodded. "So, now we know that the gun made it into someone else's hands. Granted, if it had been used on a normal robbery or some other crime, it wouldn't be an issue. The fact that a Russian with ties to funding terrorism was killed with it—that's highly problematic."

"And again, it could be just a chance meeting," TJ said.

"What do you think happened?" Del asked.

Marcus watched the myriad of emotions move over her expression. It was so slight that he doubted other people noticed.

"At this point, I'm not sure. I have a few ideas, mainly that these three were the stooges. Someone wanted it to look like they planned it themselves. Or, they were willing martyrs, although that's more of a Muslim attribute. They tend to believe in the cause. Many Russian assets are either FSB operatives or they are being blackmailed in some way, like I said. Either way, someone, or a group of people, were in charge of the bombing. Not these three, who had very low digital footprints, but none of it pointed to a clever mind. And whoever planned this attack was clever."

Del nodded. "Make sure you go over the old case files. I have no doubt you know the case forwards and backwards but looking at it now with the new evidence and the indication that Golubev might have been involved, might shake something free in your memory."

She shook her head.

"Okay, everyone, go home. Get sleep. Then come back bright and early to catch the bad guys."

"You don't want to go over the bombing—I mean the logistics of the attack?" Tamilya asked.

"No. I want everyone to get some sleep, including you. While this problem was dropped on our doorstep, there is no imminent threat that we know about. I called around to a few of my friends still working Military Intelligence and they said there is no indication of a threat, but I'm their first call if there is."

She nodded as everyone started to clear out of the conference room. She was looking at her phone and sighing.

"Something up?" Marcus asked.

She shook he head. "Naw. I'm just thinking that by the time I go over a little bit more of this info, it's going to be late and I have to drive to Kailua."

"You could stay with me," Autumn offered.

Tamilya shook her head. "Your pullout is so uncomfortable."

"You can sleep in my spare bedroom," he said before he could stop himself.

What the hell was he thinking? Having her over at his place was insanity. He knew she would probably say no, which meant she had no interest in him—like she had said before. Or, she would agree, and he would be thrown into the friend category. "That is if you have clothes."

"I do. I always keep a change of clothes, but I don't have a toothbrush or anything like that."

"I keep extras."

She blinked. "What?"

"Unused extras. When family comes to visit, someone always forgets something. I find it's easier that way than going out in the middle of the night—because my sisters don't ever realize it until then."

She nibbled on her bottom lip. He wanted to lean closer and take over the job.

"I think you should," Autumn said. "That way you know you can get some sleep and not have to rush back here in the morning."

"You're right," Tamilya said.

"Thanks, Marcus."

"No problem."

"I need to make a few calls, including to my folks so they don't freak. Nothing like being in my thirties and having to check in with my folks," she said with a self-depreciating grin.

"And we can go over some more of the case if you want," Marcus said. "I can go out and grab us something to eat, and we can work here."

They were allowed to take some work home, but certain files were deemed classified, and this was definitely going to be one of them.

"How about Zippy's?" she asked.

"Sounds good. What do you want?"

"Loco Moco. Thanks."

She walked to her office without another word, her fingers dancing over her phone.

"Tsk, Tsk," Autumn said.

"What?" Marcus asked.

"This is not a date. You know that, right?"

"It's two colleagues who are working late and eating dinner together." At least, if he kept telling himself that, he might start to believe it. He knew in his heart; he was counting it as a date...sort of. But he would deny it until his dying day.

"Listen, I threw you a bone tonight. I could have easily invited her to stay with me again and offered up my bed. I only sleep about three hours a night."

"Why doesn't that surprise me?"

She ignored Marcus' comment.

"But, if you fuck up this chance, I will hunt you down and make you cry like a baby." The menace in her voice was unmistakable.

"Is that a fact?"

She shrugged and smiled at him, looking very sure of herself. "I don't think I will have to because if you fuck up your relationship again, I have a feeling Tamilya will cut off your important bits and pieces."

Marcus wanted to deny it, but Autumn was probably right. Nope, she *was* right. "What do you think I should do this time around?"

"Don't look at me. Tamilya hasn't gossiped about you and I didn't ask. Just don't fuck it up."

Unfortunately, that was easier said than done.

Chapter Seven

By the time they made it back to Marcus' apartment, it was close to midnight. Tamilya stepped off the elevator and waited until Marcus walked forward and led her to his apartment. When she'd moved to Hawaii, she'd steered clear of him at all costs. It was hard because Dillon Securities had a few military and state contracts that had forced them to work together. Other than that, she had avoided knowing where he lived. Truthfully, not knowing was what kept her sane. She might not ever want to get involved with him again, but she knew he was a temptation she'd had problems ignoring while in DC.

He unlocked and opened his apartment door, then moved out of her way. She stepped in and blinked. It was spacious for Honolulu, but not million-dollar spacious.

"Did you rent or buy?"

"Buy. I wanted to do the renovations myself, so I found a place that needed a little work."

She turned in a circle, taking everything in. It was open concept, each room open and airy. It helped make a normally smallish apartment feel bigger. The kitchen was off to her left, with a massive six burner stove, lots of cabinets and an amazing island with a concrete top that also had four barstools. It wasn't overly big, but he had used every bit of the space to make it appear that way. There was a small dinette that seated four. The living room had comfy looking gray furniture, and there was a massive TV. All of it led out to the little balcony where he had a couple seats with a small table in between them.

"You must have a fantastic view of the sunrise."

"One of the main reasons I bought it. I could put the work in to watch the sun rise over Diamond Head."

She smiled.

"Here," he said motioning with his hand for her to follow. He led her to his guest bedroom. "There's a private bathroom and, like I said, there are toothbrushes in there in the top drawer. Towels are in the cabinet under the sink."

She stepped in behind him and watched as he made his way around the room telling her of the features. It had been a long ass day and she was exhausted. In fact, with her stomach full and her mind moving in slow motion, she should be ready to drop into bed and just forget all about the day until she had to start working again tomorrow.

Instead, she was revved up. Something had her motors humming, and she didn't think it had anything to do with work and everything to do with the man standing about half a foot from the bed.

"Tammy, are you okay?"

She opened her mouth to tell him to stop calling her Tammy, but she couldn't. Instead, she was staring at his mouth. She knew exactly what he could do with that mouth. Memories from their time together came rushing back, those things she didn't think about very often, unless she was alone in the bed.

He tilted his head to the side and said her name again before she drew herself back.

"Sorry, I'm just tired."

That wasn't a lie. Her bones were tired, and she should just want to jump into bed and slide into oblivion. But what she really wanted was to forget. To push aside all those things that she didn't want to think about right now. There was one way of doing that and it involved hot, crazy sex with Marcus. Heat flared deep in her belly as she tried to resist the need that grew more ravenous with every second that ticked by.

"Yeah, I can understand that. And we are probably in for another long day tomorrow."

She nodded and dropped her bag on the floor. She didn't want to face what was coming tomorrow. It would be soul crushing. The Virginia Star bombing was the end of a dream for her. It had blown all the years of hard work and sacrifices. She'd just really started the rise in her career, but she had fought to be taken seriously. In that one little weekend, she had lost everything she had thought was important. Now, she would have to go over it again and again. Each time she had to answer questions about it, she felt a little bit of her soul sliced away.

"Hey, Tammy, are you okay?" he asked, his voice gentle as he cupped her cheek. He brushed his thumb over her cheek and that's when she realized she was crying. Embarrassment had her gaze dropping to the ground. Tamilya Lowe didn't cry like a baby at the end of a long day—even if the day had been complete shit. She pushed everything aside and rested up to fight a new day. And if she did cry, she did it alone.

"Don't, baby," he said, his voice rolling over the sylla-bles. She loved when he called her that. It went against some of her more feminist leanings, but she had yearned to hear him call her that—especially in bed.

He slipped his fingers beneath her chin and gently urged her to look at him. He searched her eyes, as if trying to decipher her thoughts.

"What's wrong?" he asked.

"Nothing." She blew out a sigh trying to steady her nerves. "Just a long day."

"Tammy." The warning in his voice made her smile.

"It was an incredibly long day. And, I had to go over the thing that killed my FBI career. It's all been a little stressful."

Kiss me. All I need is one kiss. Even in her thoughts she was lying to herself. She knew one kiss with this man would never be enough.

Still she couldn't say the words. The one promise she had made herself was not to make this mistake again. Marcus Floyd wasn't a man you could mess around with and walk away whole. She'd learned that the hard way last time.

"It should have never happened that way. Addie should have backed you up."

She shook her head and tried to step away, but he held her chin firmly.

"No. You don't understand. That woman should have had your back. Instead, she threw you out there and left your career in shambles. You might have made mistakes, but I know you, Tammy. You were a brilliant FBI agent and you're an even better Task Force Hawaii agent. That sharp mind of yours couldn't figure it out, but you were close. Not one other person had an inkling. You were right and they were wrong."

"Not fast enough." She swallowed the lump in her throat. No one she had worked with had backed her up. They'd all walked away. If they had still been involved, Marcus would have stood behind her and backed her up.

He sighed and dropped his hand. "Believe me, I know regrets. I understand them. But I can't bear to watch you tear yourself apart. It physically makes me ill."

She frowned. "What are you talking about?"

He sighed and turned away, settling his hands on his hips. He seemed to be trying to calm himself down, but it also gave her a chance to take in the view. As much as she was upset, she didn't think she would ever be so upset that she didn't admire a man like Marcus. He was a big guy, bigger than even when they had been dating in DC. But that butt. Damn. Full, high, and she knew what it felt like to slip her hands over his flesh as he drove into her. Right now, she would like to take a big bite out of one of those cheeks.

She realized a few seconds had ticked by while she ogled him. Her face heated.

"Marcus," she said softly. "Talk to me."

He sighed. "I just can't. You're vulnerable and I can't take advantage of you."

She crossed her arms and snorted. "Don't tell me the player Marcus Floyd has rules."

He drew in his breath like he was trying to gather up his control and turned to face her.

"Last time, we didn't know what we were doing. Both of us have been through the wringer today, but especially you."

Before she could prevent it, Tamilya felt her spine

stiffen. She hated the way he said that like she wasn't able to handle the situation. Embarrassment pushed and prodded her temper.

"Just say you don't want me, Marcus. I can handle it."

She tried to step by him, but his arm snaked out, slipping around her waist and pulling her against him.

"Oof," she said, then rolled her eyes.

"You are insane if you think I don't want you."

His voice didn't sound as smooth as before. It was rough around the edges and sent a shiver of heat against her nerve endings. Jesus, just one sentence had her ready to jump his bones.

"It's hard to know what you want. I've never known."

She said it to his chest. She wasn't the kind of woman who would be embarrassed to say she wanted a man. But she was now. It had always been this way with Marcus.

"Look at me."

He demanded it now, instead of forcing her to do it. Which was more powerful? The demand? Maybe, because it showed her compliance.

"Tamilya…"

His tone was harder, even as his voice danced over the syllables.

She gritted her teeth and forced her gaze to his face. His nostrils flared, his heavy-lidded eyes seemed to darken just a bit.

"You think I don't want you?" he growled.

"What should I think? Last time we were involved, we fell into bed all the time, without a thought."

"Maybe that was the problem."

"What do you mean?" she asked, but he was already shaking his head.

"If you want to have a discussion about a relationship —beyond our work—I don't want to have it when we are both so damned tired that we can barely stand up."

"Speak for yourself," she said with a sniff. "I know an excuse when I hear one." She tried to wiggle away, but Marcus held onto her.

"It might be an excuse, but it's a good one."

She snorted and looked away. This time he slipped his hand back up to cup her face, urging her to look at him again. Before she realized what he was doing, he lowered his head to brush his mouth over hers. Once…twice… then he moved away.

"I want you, Tamilya, but we need to figure out where we're going."

"Why?"

"Because last time we burned ourselves out."

"You panicked when I said I love you."

He nodded. "We barely knew each other, and you were declaring your love for me. It freaked me out."

"And now you want to take it slow?"

"I didn't say that. I just said that we need to make sure this time we are both on the same page. Also, we're tired and on edge. This assignment was crap before all the Virginia Star issues. Now it's beyond complicated, especially for you."

He turned to leave, and she sighed.

"Marcus."

He looked back over his shoulder at her. "I won't be a way to forget work, just a release."

"You were the one who wanted to keep it casual."

"Did we ever say that? I don't think we did."

She thought back to those days, the scrambles to his

apartment or hers…and sometimes in her office. They really didn't take time to know each other. They definitely didn't talk about their future. They rarely went out on dates. In fact, they didn't really have any dates.

"Okay, but what do you want?"

He shrugged. "Not sure, but I know I don't want to be just a way to forget about work or pressure release."

She settled her hands on her hips and cocked her head to watch him. "You're serious?"

He nodded. "We fuck it up this time, and one of us will have to quit."

She sighed and nodded but said nothing else. When the door shut behind him and she was finally alone, she scrubbed a hand over her face. She sunk down on the bed and tried to figure out just what the hell was happening.

She had a stressful case, one that was already dredging up crap from the Virginia Star Mall bombing. Working with Marcus wouldn't make it any easier. The fact that he wanted to have a talk before she could use him to work off some of her excess energy…

Damn, he was right. She might have told him that she loved him in DC, but did she really believe it herself? Or was he right? Did they just jump into bed to avoid the stress of the job?

Lord knew she knew him better now than she did back then. It allowed her to look back over their short affair and realize they were both holding back. Breaking up with her had been a mistake on his part, but still, would they have lasted? Both of them had high pressure jobs—not much different than now. TFH was different than the FBI or the Capital Police where Marcus had worked at the time. There the job always came first. Del was a different kind of boss. Granted, he expected the best from them, but he also understood that family was important.

There was a soft knock on the door. "Come in," she said.

Marcus opened the door. He was holding a shirt in his hand. "I wasn't sure if you had anything to sleep in."

She smiled, rising from the bed. "Thanks." When she held it up, she shook her head. It was probably just one of his regular shirts, but it would definitely cover her without a problem. It was one of the red clay shirts that were sold at the Aloha Swap Meet.

"I appreciate it."

"Good night, Tammy."

"Good night, Marcus," she said.

He shut the door with a soft click. For long moments, she stared at the door. Then she shook herself free. Thinking about the case or the man presently driving her a little insane would get her nowhere tonight.

She needed a hot shower and a good night's sleep. The first would be easy, but she wasn't too sure about the second.

LI HAD ALWAYS BEEN a man who cleaned up his messes. The problem now was there was a woman in charge.

He wasn't a misogynist, and he had no problem working with women. This woman—she was a problem. She thought she was the one in charge. She didn't understand her place in their plans.

His phone vibrated on the table next to his bed. He knew without looking, it was her. He was the one in

Hawaii, having to lay low, to make sure that he didn't end up in a US prison, or worse, some CIA dark site. She would always be protected.

Knowing she would just keep calling, he picked up his phone and clicked it on.

"Yes?" he bit out.

A longer than normal pause before she asked, "Where the hell have you been?"

Oh, there was anger in her voice, but it was restrained. He didn't give a fuck.

"I've been laying low."

"Why are you doing that? We have a situation to plan."

God, Americans. They were a bunch of assholes. They talked in code as if they expected to be caught. No one knew what they were talking about. *The situation.*

"And I have to make sure I don't get arrested. Or was that the plan?"

He suspected as much. There had been once or twice he'd thought about turning himself in. It wasn't unheard of for spies to do that, and then get traded back to their own countries. Unfortunately, he hadn't completed his mission, so he would not get a hero's welcome back in China.

"That wasn't my plan at all. Golubev started getting antsy."

That was a lie. The Russian had been an idiot. It was amazing that he had made it out of Russia alive and, of course, it took him just a few years to get found out again. His big mouth always got him in trouble. One of the worst things about him was his arrogance. The man had thought he was an elite spy. Imbecile.

"Li?"

He said nothing as he rose from the bed and went to the sliding glass door that led out to his balcony. He could see just the outline of Diamond Head now, the glittering Waikiki lights illuminating the crater. He loved Hawaii. If he turned himself in, then got traded back to China, he wouldn't be able to return. If he didn't get traded back and turned on his counterpart, his days were numbered. Putin might have a lot of poisoning in his background, but so did the Chinese.

"We have a plan in place. You know that."

"I just want to make sure everything is in place."

"Why wouldn't it be?" he asked, irritation growing by the second.

"It's just hard logistically."

"You're the one who picked Hawaii. You never really explained that."

"The reason isn't important. You are being paid to get things in place, not ask me about motives."

Anger tinged the edges of her voice. He smiled. Pissing her off was the one joy he would get out of this day.

"Of course."

"Call me when you have the materials we need."

"When are you returning?"

"Soon. I have to wrap up a few things here."

Great. He was hoping she wasn't coming back at all.

"Okay. Anything else?"

His question came out more sarcastic than he wanted. After a moment she responded.

"No. Just make sure you answer your phone when I call."

"Of course."

Then he clicked off his phone knowing it would piss

her off that he didn't wait for a goodbye. He didn't give a damn. When he signed on to do this job, he didn't know it would go sideways so fast. As he looked at his reflection in the window, he wondered if he would make it out of this job alive.

Chapter Eight

The next morning, Marcus woke up before the sun. Nothing new for him. It happened a lot, and he liked it that way. Even on his down days. He'd rather catch a nap on his day off than sleep in. Plus, he hated waking to an alarm. Being jarred awake like that was shitty way to start the day.

He sat up in bed and rolled his shoulders. It hadn't been easy to sleep with Tamilya in the room next to his. When he finally did go to sleep, he had erotic dreams of her, mixed in with odd clues from their case.

With a groan, he slipped out of bed and stood up. Of course, his cock bounced up against his belly. The woman was more than he could handle in their earlier relationship, and she really was beginning to get to him again this many years later. If she had known how close he had been to turning around and giving her exactly what she wanted…well, let's just say he was walking a tightrope. One little stumble would throw him over the edge.

Knowing that standing there with a hard-on wasn't

helping the situation. She was just right next door after all, and he could slip into her room…

"Nope," he said to himself shaking his head. Forcing his mind away from that idea, he headed to the bathroom. It was best to get his mind off of Tamilya and on the case. To do that, he needed a shower.

Fifteen minutes later, he was showered and dressed. When he passed Tamilya's room, the door was opened so he went in search of her. The smell of coffee hit him first, so that told him she'd made coffee. His apartment wasn't that big, so it didn't take long to find her. She was on the balcony, a cup of coffee in her hand. She was sitting there, looking so lonely, as if she had to take on the entire world on her own. She had always been a solitary kind of woman, much more so than his sisters or mother. As an FBI agent, it was also odd. But he understood. Part of it was race, to a point. He'd dealt with that from time to time in law enforcement. But the bigger issue was her sex. No matter how much women had gained, it wasn't easy in any law enforcement job, especially for a black woman. They had to fight against male-dominance in the work-place, and the racism that everyone tried to deny was there.

He grabbed himself a cup of coffee and headed out to her. She turned to him as he sat down.

"I didn't wake you up, did I?"

Marcus shook his head. She wasn't wearing any makeup, and he didn't know if he had ever seen her this way. When they had been in DC, they hadn't spent time overnight together. He wanted this. The two of them together, every morning.

Damn.

"Is something wrong?" she asked.

Marcus shook his head.

"Still trying to wake up," he said sipping his coffee. The warm liquid slid down his throat. "You make good coffee."

"Why thank you, although it's really hard to make a bad cup of Kona."

"No. There is a way."

"From experience?"

"My sister was visiting, and she decided that since she knew Kona was a lighter coffee, that she would double the grinds."

Tamilya chuckled. "Good lord."

"Yeah, I think it took a week for me to get that taste out of my mouth."

"How is your family doing with you over here?"

"Mom was not happy at first, but she's been over a few times. My sister saw the opportunity as a free place to stay when they came over."

She smiled. "I'm lucky my folks are here. I would have hated to be that far apart from them."

He nodded and sat back. The first peeks of sunlight poked through the clouds and over Diamond Head.

"I can see why you like it here," she said. "I thought about renting, but I save so much money staying at Mom and Dad's."

"Nice area, Kailua."

She nodded and sipped her coffee. "Getting a little too busy these days. It was nice at first. The Obamas made it famous."

"Yeah, I can see that."

They sat in silence watching the sun rise and listening to the birds. He couldn't believe it had been only twenty-four hours since he'd talked to his mother. It seemed like a freaking week. Now he was sitting on his balcony with the one woman he thought he could never have. But now...now he wanted to be that soft place she landed. She didn't need backup, but he wanted to be that man.

"Yesterday was such a long day."

He nodded but kept his gaze on the horizon, just as she did. Again, a few moments past in comfortable silence. There hadn't been moments like this when they had their affair. It was fast and exciting and so fucking hot he almost burned up from the friction they'd created. In the end, though, it had fizzled out.

He glanced at her out of the corner of his eye. Nope. That was wrong. They didn't fizzle. He had taken a fire-hose to the relationship. He wasn't sure if they would have survived that time. Now, he wanted more, but he didn't want what they'd had.

"What is going on in that massive brain of yours?" she asked.

When he looked at her this time, her mouth curved up into a smile. Those first rays of the sun picked up the threads of red running through her hair. Even without makeup on, she was stunning. She was a woman who could turn heads no matter what.

"What?" she asked.

He realized he had been sitting there staring at her like an idiot. He couldn't help it. Since he had first found out she had moved to the island, he had that same feeling. Everything she did seemed special.

"Marcus?"

Now she sounded worried. He shook his head trying to gain control of his thoughts, but it wasn't exactly easy.

"Sorry, just admiring the view."

She nibbled on her bottom lip and he groaned.

"What now?" she asked, her tone telling him he was pushing her limits.

"That little move is sexy." Everything she did was sexy. She could burp the alphabet and he would probably think it was sexy.

"Biting my lip is sexy to you?" He nodded. "Weird."

"No. I think just about every heterosexual man would agree with me."

She rolled her eyes. "You need to get your signals straight. Either you want me, or you don't." She stood to walk back into his apartment. He should just let her go, but he couldn't let her error in thinking go unchecked.

He reached out and encircled her wrist with his fingers. So delicate, but damned tough. She stopped walking but tugged on her arm. He tightened his hold to let her know that he was serious.

"What?" she asked.

"I never said I wasn't interested, Tammy."

Her jaw flexed, but she said nothing.

"What I said was that I wanted more this time around. I don't want to let off steam and then go our separate ways. I want *more*."

She sighed and her shoulders slumped. "Okay. I get it. But what if I just want that."

His breath caught in his throat, and he felt as if his world had tilted. She had told him she loved him years ago, but now she wanted nothing more than sex? Not buying it.

"Then I guess we're at an impasse."

"Are you serious?"

"I've never been so serious in my life."

He let her go then, but said, "You're welcome to continue to use my guest room if you want to go get some clothes at your house. We might be on call a lot if something else is uncovered."

"But not your bed?"

He shook his head unable to speak. He knew he was damning himself to torture, but he couldn't help it. Plus, having Tamilya in his apartment had to be better than being separated. He'd just spend a lot of time in cold showers relieving himself.

She turned to leave, and he let her go this time. He didn't regret telling her what he wanted. It was going to suck if she didn't at least try being serious, but he didn't think he could have it any other way.

He sighed, sent a prayer to the heavens for hope, and decided to get ready for work. Sitting there sulking wasn't going to help.

TAMILYA WAS STILL FUMING when she arrived at work. Well, not really fuming, but she was irritated. The man had some nerve. She had wanted more years ago, but he had made it clear he wasn't interested. They never stayed at each other's homes, like he said. He might have chosen to leave on his own accord, but when she left, she did so because she knew he didn't want her to stay. Or had he? Had she missed the signs?

Mentally, she shook her head. He had walked out when she had said she loved him. That was when he decided to give her some space. Butthead.

She glanced at him and what she was thinking must have shown on her face. He frowned.

Before he could ask what was going on, Del walked into the conference area.

"Okay, so we have a little bit of information thanks to TJ. He's going to be in later, but he tried calling you and couldn't get hold of you."

Her phone buzzed on cue. She rolled her eyes. "Must have been in a dead zone. What did he say?"

He sighed and it sounded like the world was on his shoulders; because in a way, it was. "Nothing good. Seems that Golubev was flush with money. A lot of it. Charity is already working on the new batch of information we have acquired on him. He had accounts the FBI didn't know about, and she found quite a few avenues that the FBI missed."

"Imagine that," Marcus said as he crossed his massive arms.

"So, he was getting money from somewhere?" Tamilya asked.

Del nodded. "Bit coins. At the moment, Charity thinks it was sourced from the Chinese. Now they don't do as much as the Russians do in this situation. They tend to pay in cash, but Golubev isn't stupid. This way was easier to hide it from his FBI handlers.

Tamilya's text tone sounded and she looked at it.

Charity: Come down. I have something to show you.

"What is it?" Marcus asked.

"Charity. She has something for us."

"Let me know what she found. I've got a conference call with the mayor and governor."

"You have all the fun," Tamilya said with a chuckle.

Marcus pressed the elevator button and the door opened immediately.

Once the doors closed, he said, "Are you still mad?"

She shook her head as she went over the info Del had just told them. Golubev had money from somewhere.

Probably China, and Li was well known in terrorist circles. What would the two of them be up to?

"Earth to Tamilya."

She blinked and looked at him. "What?"

"Nothing."

"Is this about our personal life?"

He nodded.

"Not important right now. What's important is this case."

The door opened on their floor and he waited for her to step off in front of him.

"What?" he asked.

She stopped and looked at him. "If he was working with Li and he was here for a reason, then there is a good chance that Hawaii is the target. That means we might have another Virginia Star Mall bombing on our hands."

On my hands.

Her stomach tightened when she remembered the slip of paper.

"Ala Moana."

"What?" Marcus asked.

"The slip of paper said Ala Moana. It could be another hit in a mall filled with civilians."

"Could be, but remember, Golubev didn't like hitting civilians."

"But he's dead. That might have been the issue and why they killed him."

Anxiety started to pound away at her. She didn't know if she could take another serious case on that scale. Not right now with all the connections. In fact, there was a good chance she would never be able to handle a case like the again. Mentally and emotionally, she took a hit.

"Hey," he said, settling his hands on her shoulders.

She looked up at him. "We will see this through. You're at TFH and we're ohana. We don't fuck each other over to get ahead."

His gaze was steady and true and his voice confident. This is what she needed. This man with her all the time as a partner. And he was. Since she had started at TFH, Marcus and she had worked on a few things. Not once had he ever questioned her opinion, unless they were openly debating an issue. She knew that she would always be able to trust him. Her stomach muscles eased, and she drew in a deep breath, nodding.

"Thanks. I needed that."

"I could tell," he said. "I understand. The Capitol Police weren't that much different."

He was right. While a lot of people might not think it, promotions were a cutthroat situation with the Capitol Police. Even the lowest level positions were considered high profile because you had to handle political situations all the time. But it was a small police force with very few supervisory positions to be had.

"And just what is going on in here?" Charity asked smiling. Standing behind her was Autumn, who was eating what looked to be cold pizza.

"Just…nothing," Marcus said dropping his hands. She immediately felt the loss of connection.

"Marcus was just reminding me that TFH is different than the FBI."

"Thank God. You can't trust anyone who works for the federal government," Autumn said between bites.

"*You* worked for the federal government," Charity said with a laugh.

"Yeah, well, how do you think I know this?" she asked with a smirk.

Tamilya waved away their discussion. "What do you have for us?"

"Say you love me," Charity demanded.

"Charity," Marcus said.

"You should say it because it is some damned good stuff," Autumn said.

"We love you. Now tell me before I have to explain to the Hammer why you're dead," Tamilya said.

She preened a little, then said, "Oh, just video tape of the woman who was in the room with Golubev."

Chapter Nine

As Charity played the video of the woman, Tamilya's stomach tightened again, and her head started to pound.

"We don't get a good look at her face, but we do get her height, which is about five foot two—" Charity said before Autumn cut her off.

"Tiny," Autumn said, eating yet another piece of cold pizza.

"Are you eating again?" Tamilya asked.

"I just had a candy bar for breakfast so I'm hungry," she said right before taking another huge bite. Tamilya chuckled. She didn't know where Autumn put the calories she ate.

"So, yeah, back to the case," Charity said with a laugh. "She is tiny, in height but also bone structure. It irritates me that we can't get a clear view of her face."

Tamilya watched as the woman and Golubev rode up on the elevator together. It was odd that she was wearing long sleeves, a heavy-looking hat, and sunglasses. In Hawaii, the only thing that fit in the picture was the sunglasses. Most tourists would be sweating within a minute. The humidity took a while to get accustomed to and tourists rarely did. The only thing they could tell was that she was a white woman. And even that was in question. She could be using makeup on her flesh to make her appear paler than she really was.

"It has to be the killer," Autumn said.

"Yeah, or the one who lured him there," Tamilya said. "She might not have pulled the trigger, but she could be the person who had been contracted to bring him to the killer."

The view switched to the hallway where the two walked down to the room together. Golubev stopped twice to kiss her.

"That's one confident woman," Marcus said.

"Not necessarily," Tamilya said, watching as the two of them disappeared into the room.

"What do you mean?"

She tore her gaze away from the screen and looked at him. "Women who work in that kind of environment—whether she works for a government or is a freelancer—would know that her walk would indicate how she feels in the world. You're trained to walk like that. I know I was. Doesn't mean that she's a bad ass, but it could mean that she's had training."

"Me too," Autumn said finishing off her pizza. "Even when I was undercover as a crack whore—"

"Wait, you were undercover as a crack whore?" Charity asked. "We must have deets."

"No, we need to get our work done, then she can tell us. So, we don't know much about her; other than she's tiny and apparently has ice in her veins because that was mid-day and she had all of those clothes on," Tamilya said. "What about leaving the room?"

Charity shook her head. "That was messed with. I tried to go through it, but they said the disc had been wiped clean."

"So, maybe she—or whoever she's working with— thought they had all the recordings. Or, maybe she left looking like herself, so she deleted those. Either way, she can hack, or she has connections to hackers. Which, if she's a spy, makes sense. Russia has their troll farms, but China has some world class hackers working for the Ministry of State Security."

"It's more than we previously had. Plus, now that I know what she looks like, I'm going to search the feeds around Honolulu for that afternoon. We might get lucky and gather more info," Charity said. "Someone dressed like that is going to appear out of place."

"Sounds good. Ping Marcus or me if anything pops up."

"Sure thing."

"Let's go talk to Del," she said, and Marcus nodded. As they waited for the elevator, her thoughts went back to the woman. There couldn't be that many agents in the world that small. It wasn't that a woman that size wasn't capable of doing the job, but it wasn't something she saw every day.

They stepped into the elevator.

"What are you thinking?" he asked.

She broke away from her thoughts. "I'm not sure if she is an agent. I could see her being an agent in some ways, but a woman that small doesn't always make it through a lot of the training."

"But Chinese women are usually smaller in stature."

"Yeah, that's true. She had white skin, but, then again, she could have used make up to hide that."

"He had no idea she was an agent. Like it wasn't a meet up."

"What do you mean?"

"I looked at him. The expression on his face told me he was ready to get it on. The two kisses...he wanted her. So, if she was work, it was part pleasure."

"I didn't even think of looking at him. I was so intent on her," she said, irritated with herself for missing it. She rolled her shoulders trying to get herself prepared to brief Del, although now she questioned whether she knew her crap. She had missed even looking at Golubev.

"Hey," he said turning toward her. "Don't let it go to your head. You can't find everything. You missed one thing. I'm sure I missed a lot."

"No you didn't."

"I missed the skin color. I mean it registered, but I didn't factor it into whether she was white or not. I guess, like you said, it doesn't matter with the makeup and things they can do today. She was so well covered."

She nodded as the door opened. Standing on the other side were Adam and Del. They looked between the two of them, and Tamilya felt her cheeks turn warm.

"Hey, we were coming to see you," Adam said.

"Now you don't have to. We got the woman on tape," she said stepping off the elevator, causing Marcus to follow her.

"And?" Del asked.

"We know she's small, about five one or maybe five two at most. She was covered almost from top to bottom."

"What do you mean?" Adam asked.

"She wore a long-sleeved coat, a hat, and sunglasses."

"And it was damned hot on Saturday, even for locals, because the trade winds were dead," Adam said. "Anything else?"

"She looked like she was white with black hair, but these days, either of those things could be faked. Hair dye or wig would be easy enough and makeup has definitely advanced to that, especially if she's a Chinese spy. The recording for when she left the room has been wiped clean."

"So, the only thing we know is that she is small in stature."

"And we don't know if she was going there to kill him or to be the lure. Either way, she was involved. No one dresses like that in Hawaii. She knew those cameras were there. She didn't even look directly at them so we couldn't get a clear face shape."

Del nodded.

"Charity is going to take a gander at some other feeds to see if she can see something. If she wasn't a lure or the killer, then maybe she's hiding somewhere," Marcus said, but his tone told her he didn't believe his own speculation. None of them did. That was a woman on a mission.

"Sounds good."

"I'm going to do some calling around on Li. He's got a long history of not just pissing off the FBI but also the CIA and MI-6. I have a few people I can talk to."

"Sounds good."

She started to walk back to her office and noticed that Marcus didn't follow.

"I've got to talk to Del about some leave in a few weeks."

He had said his sister was getting married in Hawaii, so that made sense. As she went back to her office, she tried to put him out of her mind and work. Even back in those heady days of their affair, she could focus on work. He had never intruded in her work hours, unless she had an hour to spare. Now though, she seemed to be completely and absolutely infatuated with him.

She shut the door to her office and sat down behind her desk. She needed to get her head screwed on straight. This case was starting to give her the willies. It was too close to what happened during the lead up to the Virginia Star bombing.

With that in mind, she pulled out her cell and started to run down some leads. Maybe if they could clear up this case, she could figure out just what the hell to do about Marcus.

BY THE TIME they settled in Del's office, Marcus knew they weren't going to talk about his leave. He saw the look Adam and Del shared and knew there was going to be a discussion about his relationship with Tamilya.

"Tamilya is staying with you?" Del asked.

"She did last night—in my guest room. I offered her the room while we're handling the case."

Del leaned back in his chair, which squeaked. The sound was so damned loud as both Adam and Del studied him. They were easygoing supervisors. When Marcus worked in the Capitol Police, everything was so damned political. No one could really be at ease at work like he was here. Still, when they studied him like this, it made Marcus feel like a freaking specimen.

"So, not dating?" Adam asked.

He looked between the two of them. "No. But is it any of your business?"

"Actually, it is. If the situation does become…romantic…then you both have to file a memo saying you are dating. Kat and Drew were required to do the same."

He nodded. "No need."

Yet.

Damn, he had said he wanted something more. The easiest thing would have been to take her to bed last night. She would have come willingly, but Marcus was sure the moment Tamilya had rolled out of his bed, she would have made excuses. But he wanted more…and he wanted it with her.

"If it changes, let us know. It won't be an issue since neither of you are in the chain of command. There is another thing we wanted to talk to you about," Del said. "They want us to have more subdivisions within TFH. Not my choice. The governor wants them. And, after going over the plans, it makes a little more sense."

"And that applies to me for what reason?"

"You and Tamilya have terrorism in your background, but she has more time in domestic and international terrorism. We want her to be the point of contact for that division. She would oversee the training and the allocation of duties. Her level in TFH will stay the same so she wouldn't be your boss."

"Have you told her yet?" he asked.

Del shook his head. "We wanted to discuss it with you because you've been with us longer, and we hired you because of your background. She just has more experience."

He didn't hesitate. "And she should handle that. I'm good with on the ground kind of activities, and I can help out with planning and training. But Tamilya sees the bigger picture. She always makes connections I sometimes miss."

Adam and Del shared a look.

"What?" Marcus asked, trying to keep his temper under control. He hated being left out of the loop.

"We thought you would put up more of a fight," Adam said.

"Oh, well, no. I know both of our strengths and weaknesses. She's a good pick."

Del nodded. "Good."

"Is that all?"

"Yeah," Adam said. As Marcus rose out of his chair to leave, Del stopped him again with another announcement.

"We're going to hire this Harrington to lead up search and rescue when needed."

Damn. "That's not a problem."

"Okay good. He's the best candidate and comes highly recommended."

"Can I go now?"

Del nodded and he left both of them and headed to his office. He didn't need speculation to start growing about Tamilya and him. The last few months, the rest of the group had been betting—something Del had strictly forbidden and which they all ignored—on his relationship with Tamilya. If she knew, there was a good chance she would be pissed.

With a sigh, he sat down behind his desk and started up his computer. As he waited the few seconds it took to warm up, Marcus went over the few facts that they had figured out already. They knew the killer—or killer's helper—was a small woman, who dressed like she was an extra on a bad film noir movie. People had to have noticed her in Honolulu. It didn't mean they would get a look at her face, though. That was the one detail they were missing. He knew forensics had taken prints in the elevator, but even if they cleaned the buttons every day—and he highly doubted their claim—there were hundreds of prints. Sorting through them would take forever.

Before he could work it all out in his brain, there was a knock at his door.

"Come in," he said. Autumn opened the door and stepped into his office, shutting the door behind her.

"What's up?" he asked.

Autumn was strange, that was true, but she was a first-rate team member.

"What were you talking to the boss about?"

"They're hiring that Harrington guy."

Her eyebrows shot up. "And they were telling you because?"

"You know why they told me. Everyone knows."

"Yeah," she said, making herself at home by sitting in front of his desk. She stacked her tiny feet on top of his desk. "I don't see why it would be a problem though."

She shrugged and Marcus had to bite back a growl. The woman's mind went on trips that he didn't want to take with her.

Finally, she said, "Tamilya has no unresolved feelings for him."

"She told you that?"

She shook her head. "I saw them together. They were easy, no tension. They got along."

"We get along."

"Yeah, but there is always a sizzle between you. I get a contact high when I'm around you two."

"What do you mean?"

She opened her mouth to answer, but there was another knock at his door.

"Come in," Autumn said. The woman was really a piece of work.

The door opened and Tamilya popped her head in. Her gaze took in the scene. "Oh, I thought your voice sounded strange."

Autumn apparently found that damned funny.

"Did you need to go over anything with the case?" he asked.

"Just wanted you to know that I got hold of another CI that Adam said was good. She'll meet us this afternoon. I told her two would work."

He nodded. "Sounds good."

Then she simply stood there, and Autumn just sat in her chair. She didn't move.

"Autumn, I need to talk to Marcus," Tamilya said pointedly.

"Okay."

"Autumn, remember when you told me you wanted to know when you were being an asshole?"

"Yep." Then she looked at Tamilya and smiled. "I get it. Leaving."

She scooted around Tamilya and out the door. Tamilya shut it behind her.

"What's up?" Marcus asked.

"I thought you needed rescued."

That comment made his lips twitch. "Rescued? From Autumn?"

She sighed and walked over to take the seat that Autumn had just occupied. "Yes. I am not an idiot. These people around here bet on everything. Hell, I heard them betting on what color shirt Del was going to wear the other day."

"That had to do with if Emma and he had resolved their fight about who had to do the laundry."

One eyebrow rose in question.

He smiled. "Emma said her IQ was too high to worry about things like that."

She chuckled. "Sounds like her. Anyway, if you think Autumn was just in here to chat, she was not. She was gathering intel."

"About us?"

She nodded.

He snorted. "I didn't tell her anything…" He remembered the way she studied him. "Son of a bitch."

She laughed. "Now you know why she was so damned good at undercover."

"I think I need to have a chat with her."

She shook her head. "She'll just mess with your head even more."

"Are all DEA agents like that? I've only met a few, but I haven't really worked with them."

"No. The woman was raised by a man who was running a doomsday cult. As much as she hates him, it doesn't mean that she didn't learn her current behavior from him."

He thought it over and apparently took too long. "What?"

"I wonder if Del knows she's good at undercover?"

"I'm sure it's in her file. Not that she wants to do that anymore. She said it was too easy to lose yourself there."

"I've heard a lot of people say that about deep undercover."

"Anyway, I was going to run by my house and pick up some clothes and things."

For a second, he couldn't believe she had agreed to stay with him. Then, it hit him. She didn't say where she was going to sleep.

"Are you planning on staying with me?"

She nodded. "Unless you changed your mind."

No fucking way. "Nope."

"I figured I would be back here in time to head out for our meetup with the CI."

"Where is that?"

"Near Haleiwa."

"Why don't we go to lunch later on the way? That way you can either pick the clothes up on the way or when we head back."

For a second, she said nothing. He didn't know why she was hesitating. It wasn't like he didn't know where she lived. He'd looked it up, of course. Not in a stalker kind of manner. It wasn't like he drove by her house that often.

Damn.

"Marcus?"

He cleared his throat. "Yeah, so I think that would work better. We're going to be fighting traffic one way and it will save you some time."

She studied him for a long second, then she nodded. "Okay. Food first, then we'll stop by my house."

He felt like he had won a prize.

"I have a conference call with Addie and the head of this fubar of an operation that was used to bring in Golubev in a few minutes. Do you want to listen in?"

He wanted to say yes, but not for work reasons. If he went into her office, he could spend more time with her.

Jesus, he sounded pathetic even in his own head.

"Naw. I'm going to do a little more research on this Li guy and see if any other agencies have him on their radar, then I'll probably help Charity with the footage search."

She nodded. "I figure we can head out about eleven or so?"

"Sounds like a plan."

She slipped out the door and shut it behind her. He had a moment to sit back and gather his thoughts. It was worse than when they had dated last time. It wasn't an infatuation or just a way to blow off steam. This was full on feelings, and he knew in the end, both of them could end up hurt. But for the life of him, he couldn't give up the thought of being with her. And not just in the bedroom. He wanted more, and he had definitely finagled his way to go to her house to hopefully meet her parents.

He groaned and scrubbed a hand over his face. Never in his life had he wanted to meet the parents of one of his lovers. Just that alone should scare him, but at this point, Marcus was pretty sure it was too late.

Chapter Ten

I rritated didn't begin to describe Tamilya. She felt the entire day had been a waste, other than finding out that a woman did, indeed, go up into Golubev's room with him and exit about an hour later. They still didn't have a face, or an ethnic background for her. She seemed to have disappeared off the earth the moment she left the hotel.

The meeting with Addie had her even more agitated. She spoke down to Tamilya like she was a first-year recruit. She had always respected her former boss, but Addie had put her in her place. She knew Addie was under pressure to get any loose ends wrapped up before she retired, but Tamilya refused to be the scape goat... again. Still, she had given both of them some information to look up and maybe they would have a list of female agents who worked with Li. Hopefully, she would get a call back soon about that, but she wasn't holding her breath.

Just remembering the conversation sent her temper flaring.

"I can look for you, Tamilya, but I have a feeling you are barking up the wrong tree," Addie said.

"I think the key is the woman. She might not be an agent, but she was definitely used to get him there."

Addie said nothing, but Tamilya held her own. There was no way she was going to let Addie dictate her investigation.

"I can look for you." The tone of Addie's voice let Tamilya know she wouldn't try very hard.

"I'll put a few people on it here. That way we can eliminate the line of inquiry faster if it does turn out to be nothing."

Tamilya was still pissed. It wasn't her fault this fell into her lap again. It was really the fault of the FBI for not following up on her investigation or looking for other links after the bombing. It was also their fault Golubev was in Hawaii to begin with. If they had done their job and kept their eyes on him, the Russian would have never made it off the mainland.

And the third thing on the list, the CI. Amber had nothing for them. She could tell the woman was a junkie looking for a handout. She knew nothing about the entire mess that had been dropped in their laps.

"Stop grinding your teeth," Marcus said. She glanced over at him and then back at the road.

"I am not grinding my teeth."

He chuckled. "Sure."

"It's been a crappy day. Not one thing has helped. We have all these loose strings that we can't tie up."

"It's frustrating, but it's only the second day."

He didn't understand. Tamilya wasn't sure anyone would be able to understand what she was going through.

"No. It's been close to five years now. I've been hunting this sick bastard for five years."

There was a long beat of silence where the only sound in the SUV was stupid Willie Nelson.

"That's true."

At least he agreed with her on that. The one thing that *had* gone right was that her parents had not been at the house. She had already told them she was staying in Honolulu for work. Granted, they thought it was with Autumn. She didn't actually lie. They assumed and she let them think that. Someday she would feel guilty about it, but at the moment, she really couldn't care.

Right now, she had bigger issues on her mind than lying to her parents. Well, not really lying. She glanced over at her companion again. The fact that he was holding out was really starting to irritate her. From the moment the case had started, she had been worried about what was going on with the case. That had to be what she was most irritated about. Not the fact that she wanted to slide onto Marcus' lap and take complete advantage of his magnificent body.

She sighed and rested her head on the headrest as her eyes slid closed. She didn't need this case, or this man in her life. She needed a cool easy pace. Not a man who made her nervous—or a case that had her getting more and more anxious by the minute. In the years after leaving the FBI, she'd had some therapy to deal with the massive loss of her job. She thought she had worked through everything. Instead, she felt as if she were slipping again, becoming obsessed with the job and Marcus. Granted, she hadn't gone over the edge with the job, but the man… well, the only reason she hadn't woken up in his bed that morning was because he said no.

"What is going on in that beautiful head of yours, Tamilya?"

"Nothing," she said without opening her eyes. If he

would just shut up, she could pretend he wasn't there and the fact that it was his house she was sleeping in tonight. Alone. Dammit.

"It doesn't sound like nothing."

"Drop it, Marcus."

"I don't want to."

"We don't always get what we want," she said rubbing her temple. A headache was starting.

He said nothing else as he continued to drive. He had the windows down, which she loved, especially driving on this road. Every now and then she would smell the plumeria and it always relaxed her. At least as much as she could be relaxed driving to town with him.

He slowed down as they hit town, but she kept her eyes closed as she thought back over all the information they had. A woman was at the center of it. Was she at the center of it previously? Had she been the one pulling the strings for Virginia Star Mall?

It wasn't until they were pulling into the parking lot of his apartment complex that she finally opened her eyes.

"Where'd ya go there, Lowe?" he asked.

"Nowhere."

She wanted to think about what she had been processing. In truth, she was completely surprised that she hadn't caught a whiff of a woman involved in her earlier case. Still, in this particular case, it was only because the hotel had cameras that they'd spotted her. On the mainland, it was probably easier to hide their interactions. Also, no one linked to the bombing in Virginia had been killed before the attack. Not that she knew of, at least. She would have to do a search of unsolved deaths leading up to that bombing.

"Tamilya," Marcus said gently. She looked over at him and realized they were parked in the garage.

"Oh," she said gathering up her stuff. He got out of the SUV and came around to her side. He opened the door for her since her arms were filled.

"Thanks," she said.

He shut the door and they walked side-by-side to the elevator. When he pressed the button, the doors slid open immediately. Once they were on their way up to his apartment, he turned to her. She realized he was studying her, concern darkening his eyes.

"What?" she asked.

"You have me a little worried."

"Worried?"

He nodded. "You seem preoccupied."

She rolled her eyes. "Of course. We have a nut job woman and a Chinese dissident running around Hawaii and we don't know why."

He didn't have time to respond because the doors slid open. In fact, he said nothing else until they were in his apartment. She removed her shoes, then took her bag to the extra bedroom.

"Do you want to order something to eat?"

She nodded. "I think we should work first."

"It's going to take at least forty minutes before they can get here. You need some food in you, Tammy."

"Don't call me that."

"You didn't complain when we were dating."

"We didn't date according to you. We just hooked up."

His lips thinned into a line. Don't like it, too bad she thought with an inward smirk. The man needed to learn not to make proclamations if he couldn't deal with the ramifications.

"I didn't say that. I said we went too fast."

She scrubbed a hand over her face. "I don't want to fight, but I can't deal with this right now. I just want to work."

"And we need to eat. We can pick a place and then work until the food arrives."

That sounded reasonable, but she didn't feel like being reasonable. She wanted to be a pain in the ass. She wanted to irritate him. From his tone, she was succeeding.

"Fine. Whatever."

He sighed. "If you would just talk to me, I might be able to help, Tammy."

Dammit, he used that nickname. Again. Right after she had told him not to. "You want to know what is bothering me?"

He nodded, his gaze locked with hers. She wished she could call him an asshole, but she knew he wasn't. He was kind and supportive—more than she expected. He doted on all the women in his family. And he was a good work partner. He showed respect to everyone, especially women. Even when they were dating, she never felt disrespected, and when they had to interact on the job—even back in DC—he always backed her up. He never doubted their opinions. He might challenge them, but he never acted as if he were superior because of his gender.

Dammit. It made him so damned irresistible.

"Okay, here it goes. I have a dead Russian that seems to be linked to the case that blew up my entire FBI career. Now we have bullets that match those found at the scene of the Virginia Star Mall bombing showing up in the victim here—if you can call such an asshole a victim—and we have a woman in the mix. I'm thinking she might just be the link. Not once did we pick up on that. It was my case and I missed something. I told myself all along that I had been wronged. That the FBI are a bunch of misogynistic buttheads who had it out for me because of the major FUBAR.

Now, top all of that off with the fact that I propositioned you last night and you turned me down, it's embarrassing. You're standing there looking at me as if I am insane and all I can think about is having you strip me naked and take me against the wall...or in bed...just anywhere. You were nice enough about the fact that you don't really want me, but I can't help it. I am just a little stressed and irritated. And hungry. You were right. We should order food."

For a long moment, he stared at her. Then he blinked as if waking up from a dream.

"You think I don't want you?"

"That's what you took away from all of that?"

"I heard all of it." When she didn't respond, he said, "Tell me. Do you really think that I don't want you?"

"Just forget it." She tried to slip past him, but he grabbed her arm.

"Tell me."

The demand wasn't so nice this time. She looked up at him. There was a strange expression on his face.

"Fine, let's finish the embarrassment part of my day. I think that if you really wanted me, you would have taken me up on my offer last night. Instead, you turned away from me."

"Jesus, woman. I want a relationship. Isn't that what women want?"

"Not every woman." She did, but that didn't mean he needed to know that tidbit.

"We need to get to know each other better."

She blinked. "We *do* know each other."

"No. We didn't spend any time getting to know specifics about each other. Well, other than our favorite sexual positions."

She snorted. "Okay, here you go. I know that you come from a tightknit family. Your mom is a teacher. One sister is an egghead—your word not mine, and the other one is a lawyer. Your favorite food to eat is pulled pork sandwiches; although, I know that you've started to get a hankering for loco moco. Your favorite football team is the Jaguars, and you really don't like baseball or hockey. Also, you barely tolerate basketball. You played defense in high school, and you prefer a little whiskey in your coffee when you don't have to go in for the day."

He stared at her.

"What?"

His Adam's apple bobbed up and down as he swallowed. "You know all that?"

She nodded. "So, apparently, you just don't know about me, but I don't care. I understand that you don't find me attractive anymore. Fine."

And that made her sad. Granted, she'd been secretly lusting for him the last couple of months. More than that really. Okay, since their breakup years earlier, but she would be damned if she would admit it to him.

His hand was still wrapped around her arm. She looked down at it, then back up at him.

"Do you mind?"

"Yeah. I do."

"What?"

"You think I don't know anything about you?"

She nodded. "I know it."

"You come from a family of overachievers. All of you

are eggheads in your own way. Your father worked in security and your mother was a professor. You're not into sports, but you don't mind having it play in the background. You are living with your parents right now because you're saving up for your own place, and since your father had his heart attack a couple years ago, you want to be close. You are so fucking brilliant, although you forget that. Your name, by the way, came from your grandfather Talmadge. You went into the FBI because your father encouraged you and you wanted to do that since the time you were eleven. You give the best damned kisses a man could get, but more importantly, I know what you sound like when you come."

Her mouth dropped open and she tried to think of something to say. She couldn't even think.

"Cat got your tongue?" he said smirking down at her.

Again, she tried to formulate words, but nothing came out. His full lips curved into a smile and she felt herself melting. Like right there on the spot, she was sure she would dissolve into a puddle of lust.

He reached for her and she stepped back. She wasn't afraid of him. She was terrified of what he represented. Tamilya knew she wanted him, more than she wanted her next breath, and that should scare the hell out of her. He'd left her in a mess when he broke it off before. What would happen to her if he left her again?

Tamilya shook her head, more to herself than to him.

"The cat doesn't have your tongue?" He cocked his head and studied her. "I have a feeling you're overthinking things."

"If I don't, I'll…" …get hurt again. She couldn't say it out loud. If she did, he would have power over her.

"You'll what?" he said, moving closer.

She shook her head again.

He sighed. "You've changed your mind? That's all you have to do, Tammy. Just tell me you don't want me to take you to my room and let you take advantage of me. But tell me now so we can move on—"

She placed her hand over his mouth to stop him from saying it. Moving on wasn't an option. Not now that she was starting to fall for him all over again. She knew it was probably a mistake. Her head was telling her that much, but deep down in her soul, she wanted—needed—this. Him. Just him.

He stepped closer and slid his hand around her waist. When he dipped his head, her eyes fluttered closed. She expected a full-on sensual assault, but he didn't do that. Instead, he brushed his mouth over hers. It was the lightest of kisses, barely a kiss really. It shouldn't have her heart racing or her body shivering. But it did. Her heart beat so hard against her chest, she was sure he could hear it.

As he pulled her closer, she let go of those fears, the ones that had held her back, the ones that told her she didn't need him. She might not know what the hell was going on in her world at the moment, but the one thing she understood was that she needed him. Now.

Tamilya slid her hands up over his arms to the back of his neck. His skin was warm, the scent of him surrounding her as he shifted, and she could feel his cock hard against her stomach.

Yes! This!

She wanted to forget about everything else in the world, even if for a little while. She pressed against him and he groaned, the sound vibrating through her entire body, all the way to her soul. The sound was so primal, so basic. He deepened the kiss, invading her mouth, and she felt the little bit of control she had left being torn to shreds. Not that she had much when it came to Marcus.

He turned them so that her back was against the wall. Pressing his body completely against hers, he slipped his hands down to the waistband of her jeans. Her stomach muscles quivered when his fingers slipped beneath the fabric. With one hand, he undid the button. All the while he continued to kiss her. Her nipples pebbled as he slid his hand up her body to her breasts. The slight touch sent a vibration of heat coursing through her entire body. Damn.

He tore his mouth away long enough to grab the bottom of her t-shirt. He yanked it over her head, tossing it on the floor behind him. He bent his head, pressing soft kisses on the sensitive flesh that rose above the fabric of her bra. She quivered as he slipped down her body to his knees. With ease, he slid her jeans down her legs. Her panties soon followed and soon she stood there with nothing but her bra on.

Marcus didn't give her time to even think about how odd it was. She was almost completely naked, and he was still fully dressed. He picked her up off the floor, draping a leg over each shoulder as he used the wall to steady her.

He kissed the inside of her thigh before he buried his face between her legs. She was already so damned turned on, she was amazed she didn't lose it right then and there. His tongue danced over her slit before plunging inside of her. It was a good thing he had her legs on his shoulders. Otherwise, she was sure she would have fallen down. Again and again, he delved into her inner core, pushing her closer to completion. Just as all the tension dropped from her belly to her sex, he moved his mouth away from her.

She growled in irritation and he chuckled. He eased her legs down, then rose to his feet.

"Stop frowning, Tammy. I want you in my bed before you cum."

She didn't know how she made it on her legs. They felt like rubber as he dragged her down the hall to his room. He undid her bra, tossing it aside before he eased her back onto the mattress. Her legs were dangling off the side of the bed. Marcus stepped between them and looked like he was going to join her on the bed. She shook her head.

"What?" he asked.

"I'm naked."

His mouth curved. "I know," he said, his deep baritone rolling over the syllables.

The pressure between her legs built and she felt incredibly wet. She needed to squeeze her legs together, but Marcus stood there, unmoving, stopping her from giving herself some relief.

"I don't like being naked by myself."

He didn't hesitate. He grabbed the bottom of his shirt and stripped it over his head, throwing it behind him. When he moved again, she shook her head again and placed a hand on his bare chest. His flesh was warm, and she could feel his heart beating hard against her hand.

"The pants," she demanded, although it came out as more of a breathy whisper.

"Not a chance. Not right now. I want to take my time with you, but if I take them off, I'll want to be inside of you within seconds. So, for now, I'm going to keep them on."

Her entire body flushed with his plain talk. She'd always loved that about it him.

Then he placed a hand on either side of her head on

the mattress and kissed her. Slow, easy…luscious. It was the only word she could think of. He took her bottom lip between his teeth, gently tugging on it before opening his mouth and stealing inside. His tongue slid against hers, tangling her into the kiss. Her eyes slid closed as he pressed closer, his chest brushing against her nipples. She shivered and felt his mouth curve against hers.

He moved away, peppering her jaw with wet kisses, nipping at her flesh and then licking as he moved his way down her body. When he reached her breasts, he pulled one nipple into his mouth, his talented fingers pinching and teasing her other one. Then, he slipped further down her body, all the while kissing, nipping, and licking her body. When he reached her pussy, he settled on his knees between her legs. Placing a hand on each thigh, he pressed them further apart, his focus on her sex.

He traced her slit with his finger, the teasing gesture pulling a moan from her. She shifted her legs, wanting—needing—to press them together, but he refused to budge. Instead, he slipped a finger inside her, curling it just a bit before pulling it back out.

"Damn, you're wet, Tammy. So, hot and wet," he said, his voice even deeper than before. He added another finger, then pressed his thumb against her clit. She stood there on the cliff, wanting to jump off into pleasure, but he held back. Instead, he removed his fingers, then gave her pussy a playful pat. The small gesture sent another rush of heat though her entire body. But, when he bent forward, she felt his breath just before he pressed his mouth against her. She was even more turned on this time around, and she thought she would come right then and there. But, like before, Marcus made sure he kept every-thing teasing, just enough to push her further, but not give her the relief she desperately needed. Over and over his tongue slipped inside of her, then up to tease her clit. She moved her legs beside his head before he clamped down on them. She was at his mercy as he continued his sensuous assault.

Tamilya tried to move, tried to get a better position, but he didn't allow for it. Soon, though, he tore his mouth away and stood to take his pants off.

"Move up the bed, Tammy," he said. She didn't normally like a man giving her orders like that, but right now, she didn't care. She just wanted him, her body was shaking with need, her mind completely void of anything but the fact that she wanted him inside of her.

He grabbed a condom out of his bedside table and slipped it on before joining her on the bed, settling on the mattress between her legs. He slipped his hand beneath her ass to lift her up, while taking his cock in his other hand. She watched him, expecting a fast love making. It was what she wanted, what she needed. But instead, he entered her, slowly, inch by inch. All the while, he watched her with hooded eyes. Tamilya wanted to press her feet on the bed and force him to move faster, but the way he held her kept her from doing that. Instead, he held all the power, the control...and she wasn't sure if she liked it.

She opened her mouth to complain, to tell him to hurry up, but he pulled back out, slowly again, then pressed back inside of her again. He kept up that pace for what seemed like the longest time. He continued to build her arousal to the point that she was ready to kill to just have an orgasm. Each little move, each thrust in and out of her, teased her with pleasure, but he still didn't give it to her. Her body was a quivering mess of need as he completely covered her, his movements faster, not as precise. He nibbled on the delicate flesh just below her ear before kissing her. She tasted herself there as he slipped his hands to her legs and urged her to wrap them around his waist.

He set his hands on the mattress, rising up just slightly as he thrusted deeper, harder, faster. Her orgasm ripped through her with such force that she screamed. She shook, her body bowing up as joy filtered through her.

But he wasn't done.

Instead, he kept driving into her, pushing her further, higher. The pressure built, and another orgasm hit her before she had completely recovered from the last. As she was drifting down, she looked up at him, his eyes were boring into hers, his own need easy to see. She set her feet down on the bed and started to meet him thrust for thrust, never taking her gaze from his.

She cupped his face. "Come, Marcus. Come with me."

It seemed that was all he needed. Two more thrusts, which pushed her into another orgasm as he held himself still inside of her. Her muscles contracted around his cock, pulling him deeper and she loved it.

"Tammy," he groaned as his eyes slid shut, ecstasy stamped on his features.

Moments later he collapsed on top of her, his heart thudding against hers. He moved slightly so that all of his weight wasn't on top of her. He kissed her jaw, the tender gesture bringing tears to her eyes. She blinked them back, not wanting to get too heavy, too soon. Or ever.

"What's going on in that head now?" he asked, his voice calmer, but not any less sexy.

"Nothing."

He sighed. "Do you want to talk about it?"

"Not right now."

It was probably the stupidest move she'd made in the last few years, but she couldn't regret it. Not when her body felt like this, all loose and sated.

She had just made love to Marcus Floyd…and she was pretty damned happy about it.

Chapter Eleven

Marcus woke, his body still entwined with Tamilya's. After ordering dinner and shoveling it into their mouths, they had made love again, then drifted off together. The stress of the last couple of days, along with some healthy sex, had allowed both of them to pass out. They each apparently needed it because neither of them had stirred all night.

He squeezed her tighter. She gave out a little snore and he smiled. It was kind of cute for a woman who could bust the balls of any guy he knew—including himself.

He might have made a mistake, rushing this moment, but he couldn't regret it. It had been quicker than he wanted. He'd thought to romance her. While their time together before had been romantic at times, they never went on an actual date. Tamilya deserved that. They both did. But still, this time, their lovemaking had been different. Slower, more loving, and he liked that. He would just have to build from that.

He looked down at her again. Her head rested against his shoulder. Every time she breathed, the exhale rushed over his flesh. After all of his encounters with women, everything with Tamilya seemed more intimate, loving. Even during the first time they got together.

She shifted, then yawned, again—cute. She resembled a kitten the way she stretched, then settled against him.

"I think we need to eat," she said, her voice sleepy and sexy. It made him want to take her again. Now.

Damn. He wasn't an animal. He could control himself, right?

"Yeah, but I think we could both do with a shower," he said.

"You go ahead," she said, moving away from him.

He let her go because it took forever to get hot water in his shower. So, he went into the bathroom, started the shower, then walked back into his bedroom. She was snuggled there, hugging his pillow. Marcus stood there for several minutes watching her. The rising sun was filtered by his blinds, but it peeked through, adding a glow the room. It danced over her flesh, making her look like a fantasy made just for him. But the truth was, she didn't need the setting. She drew him no matter what.

As he felt the heat rise in the bathroom behind him, he forced himself to walk to her. He almost hated pulling her out of bed, but not when he was going to have her in the shower with him.

He placed his hands on the mattress and leaned over her.

"Come on, Tammy."

"Nope," she said, turning over to give him her back. He chuckled, then grabbed her. She squealed, then laughed as he picked her up into his arms. She wrapped her arms around his neck and settled her head against his shoulder once more. This was what was important. These moments that seemed so damned insignificant but meant the world to him. He wanted more of these, with her, for the rest of their lives.

He loved her.

In that one instant it hit him. He had thought it before, but now, the need he felt for her went beyond the sexual. There was a bond, a mutual respect, and then there was this. Even though they had rushed everything before, Marcus remembered moments like this. Was that why he freaked out last time? Probably.

"Hey, are we just going to stand here by your bed?" she asked.

"Yeah. I mean, no. Sorry."

Then he walked her to his bathroom, setting her down so she could stand. He opened the shower door and waved her in. He followed her, stepping under the spray. The hot water beat into his muscles, easing the tension he had just felt.

He opened his eyes, watching as Tamilya lathered her hands with his soap.

"I love this scent," she said, as she slid her hands over her breasts, teasing her nipples and leaving suds in her wake.

Fuck me.

"I did," she said with a smile.

It was then that he realized he'd muttered the words out loud. He continued to watch her as she slid her hands down to her pussy. His dick hardened, lengthened. Her gaze took him in and she smiled.

"Move to the side," she said. He did as she asked— how could he not. She was a lathered, bubbly fantasy, and she was just for him. No one else. He would do anything she wanted if she just let him keep looking at her.

She rinsed her hands off, then stepped back again. He stood in front of the spray as she wrapped her hand around his dick. With ease, she pumped him, her soft touch pulling a groan from him. Then, she dropped to her knees in front of him, still moving her hand over his cock. Each time she slid up, she brushed her thumb over the tip.

"Let's go back…"

But she was already shaking her head. He wanted to demand it, but he also didn't want her to stop. Instead, he settled his hands on his hips, trying to control his need. Pleasure unwound within him as she slipped her hands to his sac. She teased him slowly, and he couldn't help but think it might be some kind of payback for before. Of course, he couldn't complain when it felt so fucking good.

He let his head fall back and he closed his eyes, so he wasn't prepared to feel her mouth. His eyes shot open as he felt her tongue flick over the head of his cock. He looked down as she took just the head into her mouth. She kept her gaze locked with his as she swirled her tongue around it, again teasing him. He wanted more, he wanted to feel himself in her mouth, but he understood this was her part—her time to take control. As the water sluiced down over the two of them, she took him into her mouth, her tongue dancing over his fevered flesh.

As she slipped one hand to his ass to steady herself, she kept her hand wrapped around him, pumping his shaft every time she dragged her mouth up his cock. It was one of the most erotic things he had ever seen or felt. Her eyes slid closed, pleasure darkening them before her lids descended. Then, she sped up her actions, humming as she went. Each little move had him dancing near the edge. He grabbed at her, wanting to be inside of her when he came, but she knocked his hands away. She pulled back.

"I want this, Marcus," she said, her eyes directly challenging him.

Then, her eyes closed again as she took him back into her mouth. At that point, he lost it. He gently wrapped his hands around her neck, holding her still so that he could fuck her mouth. She didn't protest at all. Instead, she hummed again, the tiny vibrations dancing over his flesh. Harder, faster, he thrust into her mouth, reveling in the way her tongue would slide against his cock, the way she plucked at her nipples as she did. She gagged once or twice as he hit the back of her throat. With one last hard thrust, he came, closing his eyes as bliss took over him. Tamilya drank him down, humming and moaning in pleasure.

When he was finally spent, he pulled away and lifted her up. Then, he crowded her against the tiles. The smile she gave him told it all. She looked like the proverbial cat who ate the canary. He pressed his finger up in her, curling it slightly. Her eyes dilated; pleasure easy to see in the depths of her chocolate brown gaze.

He smiled as she shuddered, her entire body close already. Giving him head had turned her on that much.

Then, he got down on his knees in front of her. He didn't hesitate. He leaned forward and slipped his tongue inside of her again. The taste of her need, that musky, womanly tang, danced over his taste buds. The woman was definitely made for him. Sensual and delicious. It only took him adding a finger, along with his tongue, to push her up and over into bliss once more. She wrapped her hands around his head as she climaxed, her body shaking and his name on her lips as she came.

He stood, placing his hands against the tile on either side of her head. Leaning down, he brushed his mouth over hers. Tamilya cupped his jaw, the moment sweet and sensual. In that instant, he realized, he wasn't panicking about his feelings for her. Not ever again. He wanted this, wanted her beside him, in his bed.

He rested his forehead against hers.

"So, you are still going to feed me, right?" she asked, with enough sass to pull a chuckle from him.

"Definitely."

He opened the door and grabbed the two towels he had hanging on the rack, handing her one. He wanted to dry her off himself, but he had a feeling that they would never make it out of there if he did that. Taking the second towel, he stepped out of the shower. He made quick work of drying himself off and then walked into the bedroom. She took her time and he wondered about that. After grabbing a pair of knit boxers and slipping them on, he popped his head back in the bathroom. She was standing in the shower, holding the towel against her, seemingly lost in thought.

"Tamilya?"

She blinked and looked at him with a smile. "Sorry, I was just thinking about stuff."

"About us?"

"No."

He cocked his head. "No?"

She shook her head as she stepped out of his shower. "I was thinking about the case."

"Well, nice to know that I rocked your world so much that you are thinking about work."

Tamilya snorted. "No. I mean you did, but maybe it's allowing me to think of other things."

"Things like what?"

"There has to be something that connects the Virginia

Star to this case. I mean, at first, I had that typical knee jerk reaction when the name came up."

The tone she used made him think she was putting herself down.

"You're too hard on yourself, Tammy."

Her gaze softened. "I know, but it's the truth. There is no other way to describe what I did. But we were thinking the connection was Golubev."

"Yeah?"

"It's not. Think about it. He had sworn off that attack and turned secrets over to the FBI."

"Okay, but he seems like the logical point. Something caused him to change his mind, and it looks like it was the Virginia Star bombing."

"What if he wasn't involved this time? What if he's the patsy? Like, we didn't know he was still alive, so here he is, deader than a doornail, all these connections to other attacks. We would go down that rabbit hole looking at all of HIS connections. Li would come up right away."

"Of course."

"But what if Li and someone else—someone he had a relationship with in the past that we didn't know about— lured him here just to kill him?"

"The woman," he said as everything started sliding into place.

"Right! And, if she could convince him, she had to know that he was still alive. It had to be someone from his past."

"Is that going to be easy to find out?"

She shrugged, hung up her towel, then hurried out of the bathroom. "I need to text TJ and see if he can find that out."

"Whoa, Tammy, it's just after dawn. Maybe we get dressed and start breakfast before you bug the Hammer."

She frowned and looked up at him. "I said not to call me that."

"You didn't mind last night or this morning."

"Then is fine, not at work."

He felt his mouth twitch as he pulled out a pair of jeans. Marcus wondered if she realized how much she told him with that one line. And he liked that idea. He would have a secret name just between them. "Okay."

After stepping into his jeans, he grabbed at TFH polo. Tamilya was already halfway dressed when she picked up the phone and started texting again. After sending it, she dropped the phone on the bed and finished getting dressed. He had hoped for a little more time this morning, but they did have a big case hanging over their heads. With Tamilya's revelation, it might push the case into overdrive.

She grabbed her phone and followed him as he walked out into the kitchen. The coffee was already brewing when they stepped into the kitchen. Her phone dinged.

"TJ said they didn't have anything on record, but he's going to dig into it."

"Why didn't you ask Addie?"

She glanced up at him. "What?"

"Wouldn't she have good connections to help us?"

She sighed. The sound was so damned lonely and painful that it made him want to pull her into his arm. He didn't because he knew her so well. She wouldn't welcome the comfort right now.

"I don't trust her completely."

"Since when?"

She didn't answer right away, and she didn't look at

him either. Instead, she studied her phone as if it held the answers to everything.

"Tamilya."

She looked up at him. "Once she threw me under the bus, I haven't completely trusted her. I was sure that other people would think I was insane, but who does that to their protégé—for lack of a better word? I wouldn't. At first, it was just a little worry here and there, but over the years, I remembered things she did."

"What do you mean? Do you think she's dirty?" He hadn't thought that, but he would like it to be that way.

"No. I think she made some really shitty decisions that ended up screwing up the investigation. I realize that a lot of the clout she had at the FBI was because of who she knew, not what she did. She isn't that good of an agent."

"And that doesn't piss you off?"

"No. Wait, it did at first. I would get so angry knowing that while I made a few mistakes in the investigation, as my supervisor, she should've known more than I did. She seemed to be following my lead. Then the years went by and I realized that I was a fucking fantastic agent, but I like myself better now. There I was always worried about making mistakes."

He thought back to those days on the task force together in DC. "Hmm."

"What?"

He shrugged as he handed her a mug of coffee. "I just never saw you as anything but a badass."

She snorted as she opened the fridge and grabbed some creamer. "Yeah, well, I wasn't. Not back then. I tried to make everyone think I was, but inside I was terrified of being found out."

"And now?"

The brilliant smile she offered him made him blink. "Now I know I'm a badass."

"That you are," he said, slipping a hand around her and pulling her closer. He brushed his mouth over hers.

In the next instant, there was a rumble in the distance, something akin to thunder. It was odd because he'd only heard thunder once in the last several years living in Hawaii. He looked at Tamilya, who was frowning.

"What the hell was that?" she asked.

He shook his head as both their phones went off with alerts. When Marcus read his phone, his blood turned cold.

Explosion near Neil S. Blaisdell. Report to headquarters.

Chapter Twelve

B y the time they made it into TFH, Honolulu was a
myriad of closed streets and detours. Tamilya was
just happy that she'd stayed at Marcus' apartment. Only a
few minutes from TFH, but it still took them about thirty
minutes.

"Maybe we should have walked," Marcus said as he
pulled into their parking lot.

She glanced at him. Her companion, lover…she
inwardly sighed. She knew there were things they needed
to discuss. He wanted a serious relationship, but she wasn't
sure she could give it to him. Right now, she had this mess
sitting in front of her…them. They were both involved in
this investigation, but more of it rested on her shoulders.
Would there be room for a relationship when they
wrapped this up?

"Hey, are you okay?" he asked, his gaze searching
hers.

Tamilya nodded. "My mind is kind of melting at the
moment."

"I doubt that but keep your secrets until you're ready to tell me."

He slipped out of the SUV and she followed suit. The area was alive with activity. They were housed close to HPD and several other agencies, both federal and state. As they were walking, they heard a shout behind them. It was Del. He jogged to catch up to them.

"What's the word?" she asked as they all hurried into the building.

"Most of us are in the conference area. I'll go over it there."

She wanted to stomp her foot, but she knew it was the right thing to do. They needed to make sure not to waste time because in these situations, time could save lives.

"Good," he said, and she saw almost everyone was there. Only Elle and Graeme were missing, but they lived over on the other side of the island. It would probably take them forever to arrive.

"So, let me tell you what I know."

TJ and Detective Rome Carino, their HPD liaison, walked into headquarters just then. Del nodded to them and continued.

"A vehicle, looks to be a truck or SUV, exploded on the corner of King and Ward. The driver died in the explosion. It wasn't that much, but because of it, we've had to evacuate all civilians for a five-block radius." The area he was talking about had a lot of businesses. "And, of course, the Blaisdell is locked down. We think that was probably the target; although, we won't know for sure until we do some more digging. Right now, we're going to take direction from the FBI and HPD. They are the ones in charge of securing the area. All agencies are being given an area to set up operations. This is part of what you worked on last year, Floyd, so you know how this goes."

Marcus nodded. "Something like this will mainly be the FBI's, but HPD is second. We help out where needed, and we can start doing more investigating while we wait to be called upon."

"We're on this investigation," Autumn said. "Why wouldn't we take lead?"

Del nodded to Marcus, who took over the question. "First, we don't know if this is connected. There are a lot of assholes in the world. Second, we don't have EOD. They will be at the forefront of the investigation."

His phone dinged and he said, "I have to take this."

He walked away and Del took over again. "I know that we like to fight with other agencies sometimes, but today is about saving lives. Do either of you have any other reports of causalities?" he asked, addressing Carino and TJ.

"The driver is the only one right now, but their worry is for the homeless around the scene. There are a few areas down there where they camp out," Carino said.

TJ was reading his phone. "They found one other man nearby who is critical condition and on his way to Queen's Medical."

Marcus rejoined them. "There are teams coming in from both Kaneohe MCB and Pearl Harbor-Hickam. They will ready Schofield in case we need them. Right now they are going to help more on the perimeter."

Del nodded. "You and Tamilya head out there. Tamilya, you are the POC for the time being. When I get there, I'll take over that role. Text me our command center area when you get out there." He grabbed a set of keys and tossed them at Marcus, who caught them without a problem. "Take the truck with all the gear."

Just then, Graeme came stomping into the room.

"How the hell did you get here?" Adam asked.

"I hitched a ride with a chap from Kaneohe."

"A chap?" Tamilya asked.

He smiled. "With one of the Marine copters. They were bringing some commanders down and I pointed out I needed to be here."

"Why don't you go with Marcus and Tamilya? They are going to set up our command post.

He nodded and turned to follow the two of them out of the door.

"How's Elle?" Tamilya asked.

"She's fine. I'm happy this is her day off."

"I don't blame you."

Although for her, home would be the last place she would want to be. Of course, Elle worked a different job. And Tamilya would always want to be in the thick of things no matter what.

"Where you off to, Lowe?" Marcus asked.

"Sorry. Thinking about how our various jobs means we look at our jobs differently. I would go insane watching this on TV."

"Me too," he said as he clicked the button to unlock the doors to the truck. She went to the passenger side. As she slid across the seat to sit next to him, their legs brushed. She couldn't fight against the shiver, the need that rose up. They had too many things to worry about right now, but it was hard to ignore the attraction she had for Marcus. It was embarrassing. As he started the truck—completely oblivious to her reaction—Graeme slipped in beside her. He was on the phone.

"I didn't bloody tell you before because I didn't have time."

"Methinks the wife wasn't happy with him taking the copter ride," he said with a chuckle.

"I did not take my life into my hands. I was on board with a ton of bloody brass, so they weren't going to crash."

A laugh escaped before she could stop it. Graeme gave her a look of disgust. She covered her mouth.

"I know accidents happen. You know you get like this…"

He glanced at them.

"Never mind. I promise not to take any more trips on a helicopter."

He listened and smiled. "I love you too, Eleanora."

Then he hung up. Marcus pulled out onto the side street. One of the great things about being in an official vehicle is that they could bypass any and all roadblocks.

"So, I take it the good doctor isn't happy with you?" Marcus asked.

Graeme grumbled under his breath.

"What was that, man? I didn't understand it."

Tamilya chuckled, which earned her another glare from the surly Scot. "Not that it's any of your business but no she isn't. In fact, she read me the riot act. Said I wasn't being a responsible father."

As Marcus caught Graeme up to speed with the situation, Tamilya thought about the part of the conversation they could hear. Elle was a new mom, but there was something else there. Something adding to the stress.

"I didn't know today was a regular day off for Elle," she said when it had grown quiet.

"She's a little under the weather."

But he was looking out the window trying to avoid eye contact. The two had married not long ago while Elle was still pregnant. She hadn't been at the wedding because she barely knew the group then. What she did know was that Elle wanted more babies and they were working on borrowed time. Elle was older than Graeme.

"So, how far along is she?" Tamilya asked.

"They just had a baby," Marcus said.

But Graeme was already cussing. "Bloody hell, she's going to kill me. Doona let her know you know. We're just in the second trimester."

She nodded. "No problem."

"Congrats, Graeme," Marcus said.

"Yeah, congrats."

"Thanks. I'm not that…well, she had a hard time with the last one, so I'm worried about this one."

It was kind of sweet seeing how flustered and worried he was. The big bear was worried about his lady.

"I'm sure everything is going to be just fine," she said, rubbing his arm. "I understand wanting to have kids close together in age."

"You do?" Marcus asked.

"Yeah. It takes a lot out of you to do that, but truthfully, part of your career will always be on hold. Kids come first, right? So, you will always want to make sure that you have time for them, especially when they're little."

"Hmm," Marcus said, pulling to a stop at the next checkpoint.

As they pulled away into the final area, she realized Graeme was studying them. "What?"

"Is there anything you think you need to tell me?"

"No."

But she felt heat crawling up her neck. Marcus said nothing.

"Ah, I see the way of it. I heard you were staying with Marcus. Everyone thinks you're sleeping in his guest room."

"And everyone is going to find out about Elle's pregnancy if you don't keep your lips shut," she warned.

"Och, okay. There's no reason to be so mean."

Marcus parked in the area where most law enforcement were located.

"I'll get the table," Graeme said before he hopped out of the truck.

"That *was* mean," Marcus said with a laugh. "Would you really tell everyone?"

"Good God, no. I would never do that to Elle. I just didn't want everyone knowing about us right now. Especially since we don't, you know?"

"No. I don't know."

"*We* don't know what is up with us. The added pressure of the others knowing and the bets that are flying round...I would rather just keep it between us."

He nodded. "And you're wrong."

"Wrong about what?" she asked as he opened his door and stepped out of the pickup. She followed him.

"Wrong about not knowing what's going on with us. I *do* know."

She grabbed him by the shirt before he could pull away from her. "What are you talking about, Floyd?"

He rolled his eyes. "Do you think we have time for this?"

"You're wasting time just asking that. Tell me what you meant," she demanded from behind clenched teeth.

"I told you I wanted something serious. I said I wanted

to take my time. You pushed it. Now you're going to have to deal with me."

"Deal with you?"

"Yeah. I'm going to be around for a long time. Get used to it."

When he pulled away from her the second time, Tamilya let him go. She was too stunned by the comment. He grabbed something out of the bed of the truck and held it out to her. For a long moment, she stared at him, confused.

"Lowe, we don't have time for this," he barked.

It was exactly what she needed. She shook herself out of the stupor, grabbed the bags and started off behind Graeme. She didn't have time for him, not now…maybe not ever. Not in that serious way.

The moment she thought that, her stomach tightened. Damn. She didn't have time to be preoccupied with Marcus, their relationship, and any other idiocy that came to mind.

MARCUS WAS STILL irritated with their discussion earlier that day, but he kept his mind focused on their situation.

"So, you and Tamilya, huh?" Graeme asked.

They'd set up their tent and tables, laid out their gear, and were waiting for instructions and the rest of the team. Since EOD were still looking for bombs, the rest of them were stuck twiddling their thumbs. Marcus glanced at the mountain of a man standing next to him. He was one of the few men who could make Marcus feel normal in size. They were both over six three and weighed in the mid 200s thanks to their muscle mass.

"I don't want to talk about it."

"Worried she'll hear?"

Marcus glanced over to where Tamilya was standing. Thanks to her being the POC, she had to deal with the organizational meeting. Most people would think he'd get pissed because he was hired before her, but in truth, she was more qualified for something like this. She was also ten times better than he was at protocol and interagency BS. He had no patience for it.

He watched the group across the street from them. She wasn't just listening, she was adding her comments. Even after the crap she went through on that Virginia Star bombing, she wasn't a shrinking violet. She was bold as brass, and it was one of the things he loved about her most.

It hit him then that even just thinking about love and feelings would have given him hives a few years ago. Now…well, now, it felt…damn. Good. Really good.

"Earth to Floyd," Graeme said, snapping his fingers in front of Marcus' face.

"Damn, what the hell did you do that for?" he complained.

Graeme stepped closer and lowered his voice. "Because the rest of the team is on their way over and they will definitely pick up on it. Especially Bradford."

He glanced over his shoulder and saw that they were just a few feet away. Graeme was right. They would figure out what was going on with him if he wasn't careful.

"Hey," Adam said. The second-in-command had a grim look on his face.

"Something up?" Marcus asked. "I mean, other than the bombing?"

He shook his head. "Just heard there was one HPD causality."

Damn. Adam was one of the original locals of the team, but he had been HPD before joining TFH. Everyone knew everyone else on Oahu, and especially if you were a cop.

"Sorry," Marcus said.

"Thanks. I didn't really know Dennis, but he was a good officer by all accounts."

"Does anyone know how it happened?" he asked.

"They think he approached the vehicle out of suspicion," Adam said.

"I know it is little comfort, but he probably saved lives just by doing that," Cat mentioned. "Dennis and I went to school together."

Adam nodded.

"Any updates?" Del asked.

Marcus shook his head. "Tamilya's over there getting those right now."

"She's on her way back," Autumn said, looking over his shoulder.

He turned and caught sight of Tamilya coming over from the meeting. She walked with a purpose. It was like the first time he had ever seen her. They were in a large lecture hall, and she had stridden down the aisles like she owned the damned place. Her confidence was one of the sexiest things about her.

"You're drooling," Autumn said. He tore his gaze away from Tamilya to look at the former DEA agent.

"How could I not?" he asked honestly.

Something moved over her expression, but all she did was nod.

"Update?" Del asked.

"We're still in a holding pattern. They think Blaisdell was the target, and there is always a chance they have bombs in there already. So, we wait here until the all clear is given."

Del made a face but he nodded. He was former Special Forces with the Army, so he definitely understood the drill.

"Call your significant others and let them know that you're going to be stuck working here. Although, most of us have our SOs here. But, let others know. You'll be stuck here for hours, so best to make plans without you. Just remember, civilians cannot know the particulars. They haven't released the names of the dead, so that is all under wraps for the time being. Just explain we are here for support and you will update when you can."

Del moved over to the tent.

Marcus had already called his mother, so he followed Del over.

"Not calling Emma?"

He snorted. "She texted me and told me she'd see me whenever."

Marcus smiled. Del's wife had a genius IQ, and she worked with them every now and then.

"Had she heard anything?"

He shook his head. "She heard the report and knew procedure. She'll probably be in later after we get back. She's doing a little research."

Emma worked with game theory and other things way above Marcus' pay grade.

Autumn stepped up beside him and smiled.

"What?" he asked.

She shook her head. "Nothing. Did you call your mom?"

He nodded, but didn't ask Autumn about her family. She claimed to have no one left in the world, which made him a little sad for her. Someone shouted out Del's name and he went to talk to them. It left the two of them together

"She's calling her parents," Autumn said.

"What?"

"Tamilya. She's calling her parents. I figured you would want to look around for her but couldn't."

Was he that transparent? Yeah probably.

"Listen, I like you. I think you are good for her," she said with a smile, but it faded. She leaned in closer and up on her toes. "But, let me warn you: You hurt my friend like you did in DC, and you'll disappear, and they will *not* find the body parts."

He blinked. "Did you just threaten me?"

"Are you wearing a wire?"

He shook his head.

"Then, yes, I did. I don't have many friends, so I am protective of the ones I do have."

"Okay," he said, not completely sure if she was joking or not.

Then she smiled. "Good. Glad we understand each other."

He nodded and Adam caught his attention.

"Be right back," he said, leaving the strange woman behind. He had to get his head screwed on tight for at least a few more hours. They had too much on their plates to be fucking around.

"NO, I'M FINE," Tamilya said for at least the fifth time.

"Good, but I hate you being there," her mother said.

"That's her job," her father said.

"I know that. I just hate that she's there."

Talking to her parents on speaker phone was always fun.

"Listen, I just wanted you to know that this is going to take up a lot of my time. We don't think it's connected to my case, but I am TFH POC for it, so I have to be on site."

"You're not looking for bombs?" her mother asked. Tamilya rolled her eyes.

"No. I'm not EOD. But we are all on deck to help after they clear the nearby buildings. Listen," she said, stepping into the tent. Autumn was the only one in there. "I need to go. There's another meeting. I'll talk to you both as soon as I can."

"Okay. Keep us updated," her mother said.

"Be careful," her father said.

"I will," she said. She clicked her phone off before her mother could come up with more questions.

"Tsk, lying to your parents," Autumn said.

"It was that or my mother wanted to come to Honolulu."

Autumn's eyes widened.

"Exactly. She wanted to make something for all of us to eat."

She let out one of the belly laughs Tamilya loved hearing. "I *do* love your mother."

"Were you talking to Marcus earlier?"

She nodded.

"What about?"

"You."

"Me?"

"Yeah. I told him if he hurt you again, I'd make him disappear."

She chuckled, but Autumn stared at her, unsmiling.

"You didn't."

She crossed her arms beneath her breasts. "I did. He needed to know."

Tamilya rolled her eyes. "I told you before to stop doing that."

"I don't wanna. Besides, I think that's not a problem this time around."

"What are you talking about now?"

"He is so in looooove with you."

She felt her heart hiccup, then start beating faster. "Stop that."

Autumn shook her head. "Telling you the truth. You should have seen the way he was looking at you earlier."

All of a sudden, she was finding it hard to breathe. All the air seemed to be sucked out of her. She couldn't gain any air. Her head started to spin. She needed to get out of the tent, away from Autumn, away from the ideas she was putting in her head. Without a word, she stepped out of the tent, but of course, her friend followed her.

"Are you okay?"

She nodded, but she wasn't. They had too much on their plates to be worrying about things like that. Life outside of their case and its possible connections to this bombing were all that mattered.

"Tamilya?" Autumn asked.

Just then she saw Marcus throw back his head and laugh at something one of the HPD officers said. The sound of it, the way she wanted to capture it and replay it over and over, was almost too much. She couldn't lose herself again. Not with Marcus. Not ever.

She turned away from him and drew in a deep breath.

"Are you okay?" Autumn asked. She glanced at her friend, her best friend for all intents and purposes, and smiled.

"Yeah, just need to keep focused. This is going to be one long day," she said, then she walked back to the tent.

Nothing else mattered at the moment. Not Marcus or her feelings for him. Her career would always need to come first.

Chapter Thirteen

Hours later, Tamilya grabbed a bottle of water as she made her way from the TFH station to meet up with TJ. At the moment, they were convinced that only two bombs had detonated and three more had been found. While the building was structurally sound, everyone, with the exception of EOD, were being kept out. In the meantime, they made calls, and talked about possible motives. It wasn't that bad for the first hour. As the day had dragged on, however, it had gotten almost unbearable.

There hadn't been a claim of responsibility in the five hours since the incident had taken place. Thankfully, no other explosions had happened on the island, which pointed to an isolated incident, but the quantity of explosives told them that it was more than just an incident. It appeared they had plans for a bigger hit and that's what worried her. While everyone else thought it wasn't part of a larger attack, Tamilya did. She couldn't explain it, but something in her gut told her that whoever planned the attack wasn't the guy in the pickup.

"Hey," TJ said. "What's up with TFH?"

"Nothing. Any other information on this Solokov guy?"

He shook his head. "Not really. Just the initial info you gave us."

Alexander Solokov was a foot soldier for one of the Russian oligarchs. He'd been instrumental in the killing of a Chechen politician. Those were all the details they had on him. He hadn't been heard from in three years. Addie had been the one who'd given her the background on him.

"I called my old boss," she said.

"Addie March?"

Tamilya nodded, thinking back to the conversation. She hadn't told Addie a great deal. Just the preliminaries. Tamilya knew she had to be careful how much she held back, because she had been picking her old boss's brain. Still, she didn't trust the woman. Addie wouldn't leak to the press; plus, her reputation was stellar. After what happened last time, however, Tamilya wasn't comfortable sharing.

"Yeah. She's the one who gave me the background on Solokov. She also gave me a list of three women he knew were tight with Li, two Chinese and one American. I sent along their names to Charity."

He glanced at her, his brows furrowing. "She had it right there in front of her to talk about?"

Tamilya shook her head. "No. She called me back after about an hour. She had a file on Solokov, but it was pathetic. Just that one little tidbit."

TJ grunted and looked back at the activity around Blaisdell. "I still don't get the reasoning behind a campaign here."

"Strategic." She knew that without a doubt.

"But is Hawaii *that* strategic? These days, to an extent they are. But what is the bigger picture?"

She chewed on her bottom lip trying to figure that out. It was what had been bothering her from the beginning. Yes, Hawaii was strategic in many ways. Pearl Harbor was a big port, of course.

"It is, in a lot of ways, just like in the days leading up to our involvement in WW II."

"People don't learn, do they? Countries just keep making the same mistakes."

She knew what he was talking about. Attacking on US soil always garnered attention and a massive build up. The public didn't believe in attacking first, but they did believe in protecting what they saw as theirs. This could start another war. Maybe that was the reason behind the attack.

Marcus stepped up and heat flared. Just everywhere throughout her body. She was at work and trying to be professional, but the person she needed to pair with for work was in her head. What she wanted was to have him inside her anyway possible. This didn't happen the last time they were together. In fact, even though she had been falling for him, she hadn't been *this* preoccupied with him. Was she really in love with him all those years ago? Did she actually know him? She definitely didn't know him then as well as she did now. He had been right. They had spent most of their time together in bed, or on their way to bed...or wherever they could have sex. Now, it was different. She knew him, his family...*him*. She just knew him.

"What's going on?" he asked, his deep voice sending waves of lust through her blood. Dammit. She loved hearing it in the dark just before he thrust into her.

Her stomach tightened and her entire body lit up like the Friday night fireworks on Magic Island.

She cleared her throat but not her head. "I just got off the phone with Addie. She's digging into past cases, and she had three names for Charity to research."

He grunted. Tamilya knew he had a lot of issues with her old boss. She did too, but it didn't mean Addie couldn't be useful.

"She thinks it's going to be a bigger campaign."

"Like more attacks?" he asked."

Tamilya nodded.

"Why?" Marcus asked.

"Why what?"

"Why does she think this is the beginning? I know that Hawaii has a little strategic value, but a bombing campaign?"

She shrugged. "There are other factors. If there is a connection to China, it is more than just a strategic value. There are financial concerns, and with a lot of shipments coming through Hawaii, that could be a reason. It's also a way to leave all of the US off balance."

TJ nodded. "I still don't get that they would attack here."

"Maybe a test case?"

TJ didn't look convinced. She glanced at Marcus. He was waiting on her, letting her state her case.

"Hawaii is a microcosm, especially Oahu. Lots of people, not much land, but it would make it easier to send the island into a freak out. Terrorism is about scaring people. Imagine living here on the island with a bombing campaign going on. Inhabitants wouldn't know when they would be safe. Add in the loss in revenue because tourists don't like going to dangerous places. It would be an easy way to test out ideas."

"That's sick, and sadly, it makes sense," Marcus commented.

"There are some real sick fucks in the world," TJ said shaking his head.

"Oh, hey, looks like Charity is on the scene."

Tamilya watched—not without a little envy—TJ's face light up with joy at the sight of his wife. It was so sweet the way he seemed to melt the moment she appeared.

He rushed to greet her as Marcus stepped closer.

"What are you looking so sour about?" he asked, dipping his head close enough that she could feel his breath against her ear.

She shook her head.

"Come on. Tell me." He probably meant it as a demand, but it came out as more of a plea. That difference curled into her heart, warming her from the inside out. Helpless to resist, Tamilya turned to look at him. They were so close that she had tip her head back so she could look him in the eye.

"It's sweet. That's all."

Of course, he didn't believe her because he wasn't stupid. He shook his head. "No. That's not it."

She sighed. "She's his whole world."

She didn't mean to have her voice crack on the last word, but it did. There was no way she could deny the yearning she had for that kind of relationship.

She looked away from him, embarrassed by her need. She should be beyond that. Her career was more important, right?

"Tamilya."

She didn't acknowledge him as she watched her fellow

TFH team members gather around Charity to help her with the goodies she had brought them.

"Hey, everyone. I brought some food," she said. "Drew's family came through. They made tons of huli huli chicken and ribs, plus they loaded me down with mac salad, rice, and corn on the cob."

Drew was Cat's husband. His family's restaurants were considered some of the best on Oahu—by locals and tourists. Bags of food seemed to appear whenever they were working a case.

"Hey," Graeme yelled out. "Charity was ours first. That food is ours."

Charity laughed. "There is enough for everyone, but it did come from Drew's family business, so yeah, you guys get first dibs. It's in the car."

"Tamilya," Marcus said again. She had to force herself to look at him. He would never know how raw she was from that one sentence she had uttered. When she looked up at him, she realized that she was wrong. He did know. Understanding shone in his deep brown gaze.

She sighed. "What?"

"You talk like you will never know what that is like."

"I gave up on that a long time ago," she said. What the hell was wrong with her? They were on the site of a bombing mishap with more possible bombs to be found. Yet, she was standing there mooning after things that would just not happen for her.

"I think that you need to make sure you know what you're talking about."

"What?" she asked, completely confused by his comment. He was walking away from her. "Marcus!"

He still didn't respond. She hurried to catch up to him. "Explain yourself," She demanded.

His mouth twitched and she wanted to smack him upside the head, but she resisted—barely.

"I mean that you need to pay attention to what is right in front of you…Tammy."

Then they were too close to the team to continue the conversation. Dammit.

"Hungry?" he asked.

Tamilya's stomach rumbled, and she suddenly realized she hadn't eaten anything but a protein bar in the last three hours.

"I guess that answers my question," Marcus said with a laugh. "My stomach's been speaking to me for about an hour."

"Damn," TJ said, looking down at his phone.

"What?"

"Del said they opened the site up. That means we're going to go in. It's been cleared."

"That seems pretty fast to me," Charity said. Tamilya didn't miss her friend's worried expression. She knew Charity understood the HPD and the FBI wouldn't allow them in there if there were any concerns, but everyone who worked with law enforcement knew you didn't always find every little bomb.

"EOD found three unexploded pipe bombs, so believe me, the place has been thoroughly gone over. We wouldn't be allowed in there otherwise."

Both she and Marcus walked back over to their area. The entire team was there, except for Elle, who had gone home. With no deaths, there was no reason for their medical examiner to be hanging around.

"Hey, so they are going to have us go in teams of two. Marcus, you and Cat can team up. Tamilya, you and Graeme. Drew, I want you and Charity to go help over there," he said pointing over to where they were taking the evidence. "They need you and Charity because they know you will be good at keeping the chain of evidence in line with Federal guidelines. The FBI will start taking over a lot of the investigation. Those of you going inside, go over here to Detective Akaka. He'll let you know where they want you. Keep your lines open and keep me updated. I'll send Autumn if she gets back. She's still helping the EOD guys since she has some experience with it. Go help find the bastards who did this."

Tamilya walked beside Graeme as they approached the command center. The massive lights they brought out were being turned on now that the sun was starting to set. Akaka had a tablet he was using to keep track of everything.

"TFH, great. Okay, we need you all to start going through the smaller rooms on the first floor. We think we got everyone out of there, but we want to make sure. EOD mainly looked for bombs. Delano told me that Lowe and Floyd would lead the teams."

They both nodded.

"One team can take east and the other west, then work your way around. We're all using Station 3, so keep that open. Good luck."

They all walked to the entrance together, and the tell-tale taste of metal in her mouth told her that the bomb had been detonated near the entrance.

"Ugh, I always hate that," she said.

"If they hadn't found the bombs, I would have assumed it was a bomb just from that smell," Marcus said. "And damn, I hate that taste in my mouth."

"We'll go this way," Graeme said motioning his head to the right."

"Let us know if you find anything," Marcus said.

They walked through the hallways to the Pikake Rooms. The structure was a massive exhibition hall where anything from craft shows to MMA fights were held. The rooms they were going to look through were on the outside of the massive arena area. They were smaller and more private. It would be the perfect staging area for a hit like this.

"What I can't get is that no one is taking credit for this," Graeme said. The Scottish transplant had come to the Island and had fallen in love with the people and the location. His wife of just over a year was another transplant from the UK.

"It's not unheard of, you know. Some of them just like to screw with people."

"True. Do you have a background in this? Like you've worked cases that dealt with a terrorist who likes to bomb people."

She glanced at him and, even in the emergency lighting, she could see his expression. He wasn't being malicious, just openly honest. "A few. I'm sure you heard about the Virginia Star bombing."

He nodded. "Aye, I heard about that, but I was deployed at the time, so I missed most of it."

She nodded. "I was tracking them."

"Them? I thought they caught one?"

"I always thought there was someone else. Popov wasn't a planner or a leader. He was a soldier recruited by someone else. There was no way he did that on his own."

He nodded as they reached the Pikake room. "Is that how you met Marcus?"

"Not that case in particular. We had been on a task

force together about six months earlier. He worked on the Capitol Police when I was with the FBI."

"Ah."

He signaled that he would take the right side of the room and she nodded. They both drew their weapons and entered to find the room completely empty. There were a few tables, but if there had been anyone hiding in there, they were long gone. They looked over the things left scattered on the tables. At first, it all appeared to be some kind of crafts, but then she saw the wires and the fine black particles.

"Damn, this is where the perpetrators were hiding before they planted the bombs," she said. Graeme was already calling it in.

She heard Akaka tell them to step away and the FBI would join them. That meant they would handle the evidence. Her palms itched and she had to force herself to leave the room. This is what she had lived for at one time, but now, she was just a grunt doing a little bit of investigating.

Oh, damn, that sounded bad.

"I'm irritated too," Graeme said to her.

She glanced at the massive man and smiled. "I didn't know it showed."

"Not that easily, but I have a keen eye. Or so my wife tells me."

She smiled. Another burly man who melted at just talking about his wife.

TJ came in with a bevy of FBI agents. Most of them looked like they might have been in college just last week. And great, now she felt old.

"Thanks, Tamilya. Good find."

"There's a lot of material in the room."

He nodded and turned back to get to work in the room. Agents were carrying in evidence bags and collection tools, and she ground her teeth.

"Let's get going," she said.

"Aye. The sooner we go through these rooms, the sooner we can both head home."

"SO, YOU AND TAMILYA?" Cat said. She wasn't good at small talk. He hated to say it, but she was like one of the guys.

"Go ahead," he said, as he walked over to the other side of the room.

"Well, how long did you date?"

He glanced over his shoulder at her. Cat Kalakau looked diminutive and sweet. Athletic, with a girl next door quality about her, she could fool any suspect with those dimples of hers. In the end, though, it would be their downfall. She was one woman he thought could probably kick his ass. She was also an expert sniper and could outshoot everyone else on the team.

"Six weeks."

"Not long."

He shook his head. "We both had high stress jobs, and she was just beginning to hunt for the guy who would eventually blow up the Virginia Star Mall."

"Ah, makes sense."

"So, have you set a date yet?"

Drew and Cat had eloped to Vegas, but their families were insisting on a ceremony.

"Nope. There doesn't seem to be anything in here."

He nodded. He heard footsteps and drew his gun, keeping it low and to the ground."

"Marcus?" Tamilya called out.

"Yeah." He stepped into the doorway.

"We found a bunch of material over there in the Pikake Room."

"Where is it?"

"The FBI is handling it. Looked like some kind of gun powder. Some wires."

"You think someone put them together here?" he asked.

"It would take a big set of bollocks to do that," Graeme said.

"Or, it could be someone really stupid," Tamilya said. "Or even someone who got off on the added danger of making the bombs here. And, then there is the possibility that the person has no other place to make the bombs."

"So they could have taken advantage of the empty rooms," Marcus said.

"And that means whoever the person is, he knows what's going on here. They could possibly have someone on the inside," Cat said.

"Yeah." Tamilya thought it over and felt the need to push her way into the investigation. Her fingers practically tingled as she gripped her gun harder. She hadn't really missed much at the FBI. The office politics and the long hours sucked. But this she had been good at. She knew just how to lead an investigation, and she definitely understood the mind of a terrorist. At least one that liked to blow shit up.

"Tamilya?"

She looked up at Marcus. "I think we're done here."

He nodded.

He unhooked his walkie-talkie from his belt. "TFH here. We're done with the search. Anything else you want us to do?"

"Come on back out here. I'm going to check in with my section chiefs."

"Ten-four."

"Well, you heard him. That means after an hour of being in here, we get to eat, or at least grab and go."

"Thank God," Cat said.

They walked together out the door and he glanced at Tamilya.

"Are you okay?"

She nodded. "Just damned hungry."

"I hear you."

They made their way out to the TFH tent where Del was eating.

"You're still eating, man?" Marcus said with a laugh.

"Just started. They made me go talk to the cameras."

"Aw, boss, the media loves you," Adam said, he looked at Tamilya and Marcus. "Grab some food, then go on over to the concert hall. They want to do a more careful search over there. All that seating is making it difficult."

"I'll do anything as long as I get something to eat," Tamilya said.

They lined up, filled their plates. It didn't take them long to finish and be on their way. They kept their teams as Del had ordered and headed off to work. He just hoped that, in the end, this was just some idiot with too much time on his hands and gunpowder to spare.

It was well after midnight as they drove back to TFH.

They'd found little evidence, other than the haul she and Graeme had found earlier in that first room. As far as she knew, no one had stepped forward to take credit for the attack.

"I'm going to sleep for a bloody week," Graeme said.

She laughed as she heard her phone ping with a text.

Are you home? Are you dead? This is your mother.

There was no way to hide the news from her parents, and they weren't intrusive, but she hadn't updated them in a few hours.

Not home. Not dead. This is your daughter.

Smartass. Love you.

Love you.

"Family?" he asked.

"Yeah, my mom. I thought she would be in bed, but I should have known better. Did you talk to your mom?"

He nodded. "Elle's been keeping her updated, along with her parents."

He yawned and stretched his arms over his head. "I'm getting too bloody old for this."

"Never," she said, then yawned herself. He started laughing.

"What's so funny?" Autumn asked as she walked into the room.

"Nothing. We're just tired."

"I completely understand that. I think we're all a little punch drunk from the day."

Marcus returned with Adam.

"So, Del said no one needs to come in until after ten unless the FBI requests us. I assume they will do most of the investigation, but they might need back up. Also, we're going to need you two," Adam said talking to Tamilya and

Marcus, "to go make sure there are no links. At least when they give us any evidence."

Her phone pinged again, and she assumed it was her mother, so she pulled it out and almost dropped the phone when she read the message.

Today, no one died. You will not be so lucky next time and it will be all your fault because you didn't stop me in Virginia.

Chapter Fourteen

For a long moment, Tamilya stood frozen, her brain unable to process what the message meant. Words were like gibberish to her. She understood what the message said, but she couldn't get her brain to compute and react. Ice stole over her, leaving her feeling as if she were encased in an iceberg. She couldn't say or do anything. That iciness slipped beneath her flesh and she started to shake. It was just like Virginia Star all over again. She was going to fail.

Then, in a split instant, she snapped out of it. She would *not* fail, and no coward hiding in the shadows was going to convince her either. She shook her head to clear out the recriminations and read the message again.

"Marcus," she said, showing him her screen.

"What the hell?"

She walked over to the conference table and everyone followed suit. She set the phone down and heard Marcus on his own phone calling in her number so they could get a trace.

"It'll be a burner, I'm sure of it," Autumn said. Tamilya felt her friend pat her shoulder.

"Yeah, but we might be able to get something anyway."

Autumn's phone buzzed.

"What?" she barked, but she smiled when whoever talked on the other end of the line apparently gave her hell.

"I'm not rude. I'm abrupt."

Another round of listening as Tamilya tried to hold onto her patience. It was a difficult task because Autumn gave them no indication as to what the call was about.

"Okay." Autumn held her phone out to Tamilya. "Charity."

"Do you have some kind of sixth sense?'

"No," Charity said, but she didn't laugh. Her tone was serious, one she rarely heard from the tech. "Autumn texted me."

Tamilya hadn't even noticed her friend sending a text. "What do you need?"

"Nothing much. Just wanted to know if this was an issue in the last case?"

"No. We had no contact before the incident."

"Hmm, so this is a change in behavior." Even on the phone, Tamilya could almost sense Charity's mind humming along as she made a few connections. She heard Charity tapping on keys.

"We don't know if it is the same person."

"Aha!" Autumn said, pumping her fist in the air.

"What was that?" Charity asked.

Tamilya clicked on the speaker. "Putting you on for everyone to hear. And so you know, the idiotic noise you just heard was Autumn."

"I knew that the FBI thought there were others involved," Autumn said. "That mall hit was too extensive for one person."

"The FBI does not think there were other people. There was no sign of it," Tamilya said, reciting the line they had all been forced to use. Truthfully, the others were happy to use it. Whether they were happy she had been left to blame for the bombing or they believed the FBI's official stance.

"But you do," Autumn said. "If you could see her expression, you would agree with what I'm saying."

"I agree with that assessment too," Marcus said from behind her.

Surprised, she glanced at him.

"What? I knew you were right. Anyone with half a mind could read your reports leading up to the attack and know you understood the real story."

"We have to look at this as if it is someone the FBI missed or someone new who could be using your connection to both cases to screw with us," Charity said.

"Always a possibility. Just so you know, TJ and I are on our own over there. We were still at the site when Autumn's text came in."

"Okay. And I am assuming that Del is on his way back?"

"I'm here," he said, walking through the doors, followed by his diminutive wife Emma. Their baby was nowhere to be found. "Mom is visiting, and I figured this might be something we need to hire Emma for."

"You should always consider me first," Emma said. A genius with questionable social skills, Emma had been working for the TFH when she and Del started dating.

"Love, I always consider you first," Del said.

"I'm the one who could figure this out, with the help of Tamilya. Now tell me what you have and what you know, and we can start trying piece together who this bastard is."

"We need to contact the FBI," Tamilya said.

"Why do we need those wankers here?" Emma asked.

"Hey," TJ said from the phone.

"Who was that? Is that Hammer?" she asked as she stepped closer to Tamilya. "Do we need Charity right now?"

Tamilya shook her head. "She's on her way back."

"Okay." She grabbed the phone out of Tamilya's hands and said, "See you when you get here." Then she clicked it off.

"Emma," Del said."

"Whose is this?" she asked. Autumn raised her hand and she handed it to her. "What? We don't have time. Those FBI assholes will show up and try to take over our case. They cocked up the first investigation—everyone except Tamilya here."

Warmth spread through her chest. "I was the main person on the team in charge of that investigation."

"And I read your reports."

Tamilya cocked her head. The public had gotten the official story, but they had not been given her theories. That had been classified at the highest levels of government.

"Emma," Del said again, embarrassment in his voice. "Tell me you didn't hack into the files to read them."

"Okay, I won't."

He mumbled under his breath, but she continued on. "I know what you were up against, and we will have the issue again, along with more problems. They will zero in on you. The Hammer might not think it, but I can assure you his idiot coworkers will."

Then, everything she said started to fall into place. "They'll think it was me. Or that I am helping with it to get back at them."

"Or a hero kind of thing where you can step in and save the day," she said. "Stupid, because you would never do that. Anyone who has read your…never mind about that."

She knew what Emma was about to say. Her mental fitness had been questioned after she'd left the FBI. It didn't stop them from calling her in again and again. She had been lucky that Conner Dillon hadn't had a problem with it and fired her. And again, Emma shouldn't have gotten that information.

Del looked between the two of them and rolled his eyes. Before he could respond, Charity came barreling in ahead of her husband.

"So, what did we decide?" she asked, out of breath.

"We have to call the FBI. This is their case."

She nodded. "I'll get started on tracing the message so we can tell them it's a burner before they waste time."

"They'll still waste time," Emma said.

"But we'll know," Charity said. "Coming with?" she asked Emma.

"Yeah, why not? When you call the FBI, tell them to get bent," she said to Del.

"Hey," TJ said laughing.

"Can you take care of that?" Del asked TJ. "I need to talk to Tamilya."

Marcus bristled next to her, but she would not have him fighting her battles.

"Of course."

She followed him into his office, and he dropped down in his chair. "Close the door and sit down. It's been one long ass day, and I am too tired to watch you stand."

She smiled and did as he ordered.

"I know that you didn't have anything to do with this, but the FBI will ask if I questioned you. Did you?"

"Have anything to do with this bombing or the Virginia Star bombing? No. Other than investigating."

He sighed. "Good. I know you didn't, but those assholes...don't tell Emma I said that. She would rather I never talk to any of them other than TJ, but that, of course, screws with my job."

"No problem."

"My other reason for bringing you in here is to talk about how they zeroed in on you."

"What do you mean?"

"There were hundreds of FBI agents who worked on that case. Only the insiders would know you were thrown to the wolves and that you took it so personally."

She blinked. "Damn. You're right. Anyone with access to the case, but that requires top level clearance. Or your wife, apparently."

"That woman," he said with equal parts annoyance and admiration.

"You could have asked me out there."

"I didn't want comments from the peanut gallery."

Tamilya found her first real chuckle since getting the text. "True."

"Plus, I didn't want to reprimand Marcus for threatening me."

"What?"

"He's watching us like he wants to beat me up."

She turned and found him standing there, his arms

crossed over his massive chest, staring at them. She shouldn't be so damned turned on, but she was. Still, it irritated her all the same.

When she turned back around, she found Del watching her. "Please, don't worry about that. About him. This is my job and I would rather not be handled with kid gloves."

Del studied her for a few moments as if trying to figure out what she was saying. "This isn't about handling you with kid gloves. This is about protecting my people."

"I don't need protection. I'm not a green recruit who doesn't understand how things go."

His expression softened slightly. "That's not what I meant. You're one of us. I have your back. I will never leave you out there on your own, even if you did fuck up. Your fuck ups are mine because I'm your boss. Simple as that."

She sighed as relief filtered through her. "Thanks. It's…"

"I get it," he said when she didn't continue. Something caught his attention, and she turned around again. She recognized the two men standing there.

The FBI had arrived.

AN HOUR LATER, Marcus was beyond irritated. Hell, he was fucking furious. They were still stuck at TFH while going over things with the FBI and TFH. He didn't like that.

Tamilya had been put in a room for questioning.

"I still call bullshit," he grumbled.

"I agree, but at least this way, they can never say that

she didn't alert them when it happened," Autumn said. Then she leaned closer and lowered her voice. "You can never trust the government."

He glanced at her. "Uh, you work for the government. Hell, you were a DEA agent."

"Doesn't mean I trusted them."

He scrubbed his hands over this face as he fought back a laugh.

"You are one of a kind, Bradford."

"Yeah, I know. And now you don't look like you want to go beat up that Agent Howard."

He dropped his hands. "What?"

"You looked like you wanted to go tear off Agent Howard's arms and then beat him with them. I was just trying to save you. Plus, Tamilya would be pissed that you didn't think she could handle all of this."

He snorted. "That woman could take on the Chinese Army without a problem."

"True. And it looks like they're wrapping things up. Are you taking her home?"

"Why would I change that?" Del had sent Cat over to keep an eye on her parents because they were now also a target.

"She's coming home with me. Del made noises about a safe house."

She shook her head. "Useless. If they know us, they know our safe houses. I would put my stock in someone at the FBI. They would be the ones who would know what was going on."

"There's one thing we have to consider," he said, watching the exchange between Tamilya and TJ. Relaxed. She was completely unfazed by the questioning that had gone on for over an hour.

"What's that?" Autumn asked.

"There's a chance they paid for a hack."

"Hmm, but still, why go after the Virginia Star bombing? Why that one?"

"There were people who didn't get caught. Maybe they wanted to find out just what the FBI thought. They gather information and realize Tamilya was here in Hawaii. She's perfect."

"Why not that bitch March?" she asked.

He looked at Autumn with one eyebrow raised. "Nasty words for someone you never met."

"The woman let Tamilya down and, let's be honest, both of us are not good enough to be friends with Tamilya. UC for the DEA makes me kind of…well, dirty. Not in a way that I broke any laws, but you have to skirt the edge. And, well, you fucked up bad with her last time."

He sighed and rubbed the back of his neck. That much was true. Before he could respond, the door opened up. Agent Smith came out, followed by TJ. Tamilya stood alone in the room.

"Oh, hey," TJ said with a smile. "Smith, this is Marcus Floyd, Tamilya's…I guess you two are partners on this case?"

Marcus nodded. Smith eyed him. He was typical of what Marcus was accustomed to in an FBI agent. Dressed in a suit, he was out of place. Granted, TJ did the same, but he rarely wore jackets these days and often had the most outrageous ties—probably from his wife. Smith was looking to get ahead, and he wouldn't think twice about tossing Tamilya over the side to climb up the ladder.

"You know you're obligated to tell us anything you might know."

"I know that you're an asshole. How about that?"

Someone snorted behind him, and he knew it was Autumn.

Smith glowered at Marcus. "You have—"

"Yeah, yeah. I know. Blah, blah. I was dealing with the FBI before you got out of Quantico, Smith. There will be no reason for me to contact you about Tamilya. The only life she would put in danger is her own."

And that was what was freaking him out. If the bomber had zeroed in on Tamilya, she might not play reckless with the public's safety, but Marcus knew she would sacrifice herself to get the bastard behind this.

"Hammer, are you coming along?" Smith asked.

"Naw, you go ahead. I have some meetings to attend."

Smith nodded and walked away.

"You're a liar," Autumn said. "And not even a good one at that."

"Whatever do you mean, Bradford?" he asked. Then he turned to Marcus. "You saw it, and she handled it fine, but I think it's been one long day for her."

Marcus nodded and stepped around him to go into interrogation. He hit the speaker button and tossed a look in their direction before stepping into the room and shutting the door behind him.

Tamilya started at the sound and turned. She smiled and relaxed when she saw him. "Hey."

"Hey, yourself. Ready?"

She nodded. "Although…"

"Don't even think about going to your parents' home."

She frowned. "Of course not. I wouldn't put them at any more risk. I was thinking maybe it would be best to stay here."

He blinked. "Here? At TFH?"

"Yeah. How much safer can I get than here?"

What she said made sense. TFH could be a target, but it wouldn't be easy now with the added security. When he didn't say anything, she continued.

"There's showers, and I know they have some decent cots. We would just have to go back to your apartment. Although," she said eyeing me. "I'm not sure you could fit on any cot they have here."

He felt his heart settled at the comment. She wasn't tossing him away. Instead, she was looking for both of them to be here at headquarters. It would make it difficult to seduce her, but she would be safe.

"I bet I can manage," he said.

"Good, then we can go to the apartment and get our stuff."

He nodded. She stood and he followed her out of the room, too relieved to complain that being at TFH would make having sex almost impossible. *Almost* was the key word. When they stepped into the hallway, TJ was frowning.

"What now?" Tamilya asked. "Damn, that sounded whiney. Sorry. What's up?"

He shook his head. "I just got off the phone with one of my coworkers."

"Not another bomb?" Tamilya asked.

TJ shook his head. "Addie March is on her way to Hawaii."

Chapter Fifteen

Later that night—or was it the morning?— Tamilya pulled a t-shirt over her head and then grabbed her sleep shorts. She was still blindsided by the news of Addie showing up at TFH. It was enough that she had to deal with someone taunting her, but to have Addie there…it would bring up too many emotions. And why hadn't she told Tamilya? Addie didn't really owe her. All right, she *did* owe her. That woman let Tamilya take the hit on her career rather than protecting her. Del had made it clear that no one would do that to her here. She'd been at TFH less than a year, but she trusted them more than anyone at the FBI. Now she was going to have to handle her former boss popping in.

Tamilya hadn't come face-to-face with Addie since her last day as an FBI agent. She had talked via text and by phone, but Tamilya had made sure to avoid being in her presence. She just didn't have it in her to forget everything. Addie was an attention seeking agent. Most FBI agents liked to be in the background. They would rather not have their face on TV, but then there were others. Those who wanted to move up through the ranks of the DOJ. Addie was definitely in that category. Now that she was leaving the FBI, she would definitely be looking to make a name for herself before her last day. Tamilya understood the reason Addie was coming to Hawaii, and it could certainly screw up their case.

There was no doubt in Tamilya's mind that Addie was going to try and take over things once she got on the island. She had seen her former boss do the same kind of thing before. More than once she had taken credit for the work of others. Not once did she ever credit Tamilya when both of them knew that she had been the one to do all the research.

Add in Marcus, and she had a lot on her plate. He was in her head too much. She knew he was pissed on several levels, most of them having to do with what he saw as her mistreatment by the FBI. Truth was, she had been where Agent Smith had been more than once. She would have done the same thing. It was the only way to make sure that you got all the facts. Marcus knew that. He'd been a cop for too long not to understand that part of the job. She could go toe-to-toe with any interrogator. But for some reason, he wanted to protect her from it all. It was like he thought she was weak.

She bristled at the thought. The idea that anyone would think she was weak was enough to piss her off. But there was another problem. Sex and work rarely worked out well. The idea that he wanted her to be with him, to have a serious relationship, had her stomach clenching. She had wanted that at one time, but now…she wasn't exactly sure. Working together wasn't going to be good for that either. Especially since they had a bit of the same background.

There was a knock at the door, and she stared at it. "Tamilya?"

She knew it would be him, but now she didn't know what to say or do. If she let him in, would he press for a discussion about their relationship? She rolled her eyes. Now she sounded like an idiot. Marcus was all about work and that would come first. With the terrorist connecting everything from Virginia Star to now, they had a huge case on their hands.

She walked to the door and opened it…then lost her breath. He had showered and was wearing nothing but a pair of shorts. She was pretty damn sure he was going commando too. She wanted to slip her fingers beneath the waistband just to prove her theory. Who was she fooling? She wanted to do it for purely carnal reasons. And he knew what she was thinking from the way his nostrils flared. He definitely wasn't making it easy on her tonight.

"What?" she asked, her voice a little more frigid than she had wanted it to sound. It was her only defense to the temptation he offered her.

If she were honest with herself, Marcus didn't need to be standing in front of her half naked for her to want him. She'd never been an overly sexual person…until she had met him. And it was *only* him. She'd had one other partner in between her two relationships with Marcus, and she hadn't been this obsessed with sex with Harry.

"I'm gonna bring this in here," he said, motioning to the cot next to him. Yeah, there was that too. She didn't seem to even notice anything but Marcus when he was around. And that was a problem for an agent.

"I don't see why you'd have to sleep in here."

He studied her for a long moment, then shook his

head. "It's not for what you think. I want to be between you and the door."

"I can protect myself."

"Yeah, but more than one of us can take anyone who shows up."

Well, damn. She had to admit—only to herself once more—that she was a little disappointed. He must have sensed it because he leaned closer to whisper.

"You know there are cameras everywhere in this building. I don't mind people knowing about us, but I definitely don't want to be worrying about our escapades being filmed and reviewed."

Her face heated as his mouth brushed against her cheek, then he pulled back.

The intimate moment, the little butterfly kiss, had her head spinning. Hell, she didn't have to look down to see that her nipples were hard.

"Tammy?"

"Hmm?"

"Could you move so I can wheel this in there?" he asked, motioning to the cot again.

"Uh, yeah, okay," she said, stepping back and letting him into her office. She moved away from the door and tried to calm her nerves. He was right. There was no way to get away with sex at work. It was unprofessional and definitely a big *no* from her. But why did the idea make her panties wet?

Because the man was driving her insane. Seriously. Last time had been bad enough, but this time it was beyond that primal need they had for each other. Now, though, there were those moments where he made her believe this would be more. He made it sound like he wanted a relationship with dates and commitments.

She squashed that idea. She didn't need to be betrayed again by what her mother called her soft heart. Tamilya hid it for a variety of reasons. Being an FBI agent and being female was always difficult. Being black…magnified that difficulty. She couldn't show any weaknesses—more so than any of her male counterparts. Then, Marcus had happened and then the bombing had happened. That had pushed her over the edge, and she had promised herself to never again lose her composure.

She watched as he wheeled his cot into her office. She knew resisting him now would be complicated, and her body truly didn't want to. If she couldn't resist him, she would just have to do her best to keep from falling for him again.

Just then, he glanced over his shoulder at her and smiled. Her heart ticked up a couple beats and her entire body was flooded with heat. It wound through her blood making her mouth water and her panties even damper.

Resisting him was definitely easier said than done.

MARCUS GROANED when he turned over in the cot and had the sun splashed directly into his eyes.

"Fuck," he said.

"Dirty mouth," Tamilya said from behind him.

"Easy for you to say. My body is shielding the sun."

She giggled. It was so light-hearted that his entire body reacted. Heart, soul, and of course, his cock. Where Tamilya was concerned, he would always react that way. Hell, he worried that she might just raise him from the dead if she attended his funeral.

He turned back over to face her. She was laying on her

back, her eyes closed, and a small smile playing about her mouth.

"How did you sleep?" he asked.

She shrugged. "Okay considering. My mind took a while to calm down."

He nodded, watching her for a long moment, then he realized she couldn't see his nod with her eyes closed.

"Yeah, me too."

Her eyes flickered open and she glanced him. He wanted this. Not in the TFH headquarters, but he wanted her by his side, waking up every day. She had a dark green scarf on her head and her eyes were heavy with sleep. The tank top she was wearing molded to her breasts, and he knew from his brief view last night, she wasn't wearing a bra. He wanted to slip his hands down her body and beneath the waistband of her shorts to see if she was wearing any panties.

He tried his best to push that thought away, but with his early morning erection wanting attention, it wasn't easy. Neither of them had had much sleep last night or the night before. They were both going to feel it today.

"What?"

He shook his head. "I don't know if any woman could look this stunning after the last few days."

She rolled her eyes. He hated that she didn't believe him. It was one of the things during their short relationship that had irritated him. He was starting to understand it now. Tamilya wanted to be accepted for her intelligence and work.

"You are, but you could have a bag over your head, and I would still think that. Mainly because the whole package is what draws me in."

"Yeah, I've always known you were a boob and butt man."

He chuckled at her terms. Tamilya would never say tits and ass.

"Nope, that's not it." She let one sculpted eyebrow rise up. "Oh, I do like your body, but you know what always got me hot? Your mind."

She rolled her eyes again.

"No. Really. The first time I saw you was at a briefing. You didn't have to use your notes. It was all up here," he said touching her forehead. "That mind is a dangerous thing."

She looked like she wanted to believe him, but Marcus could tell she wasn't convinced.

"I could get a lot of women."

"Well, I'm glad you can brag about that."

The sarcasm and jealousy he heard then tugged a smile out of him.

"You know what a uniform does to women." There were always women who hung out at cop bars trying to hook up. "But there I was in a briefing room, FBI, Capital Police, and a bunch of Homeland Security assholes, and I got hard."

"What?"

"Serious as a heart attack. You got up there and that one dweeb Anderson from Homeland kept trying to mess with you, and you shot him down over and over. It was a thing of beauty," he said, not able to keep the admiration out of his voice. She'd been outnumbered by the attendees by sex and skin color and she didn't give a damn. She destroyed every argument Anderson had tried to throw at her. "I knew by the end of the presentation I had to have you."

And he had. He had approached her afterward, said he wanted to pick her mind about something, and they had ended up in bed less than two hours later. He was getting so damned hard thinking about it right now. Not just her sex. Her brain was one of her most alluring attributes.

He cupped her face.

"You're the whole package, Tamilya."

"It won't work. *We* won't work."

He heard the doubt in her voice, but it also sounded like she was trying to convince herself. There was also a thread of pain lacing her words. He hated that it was between them, the memories of him being a coward. He knew he hurt her, and it was his own damned fault she didn't trust him. He would just have to spend the rest of their lives proving he was worth the effort.

"We could try."

Her mouth thinned and he knew that he had touched a nerve. He wanted her to say that everything would be okay, that they would get their own happily ever after, but he didn't want to force anything. He also didn't want her freaking out and running the other direction. That's what he'd done the first time around. So he knew he had to be patient.

"We have too much on our plates to worry about it right now. Just…wait until you make a decision. I would rather you not have a mad bomber threatening you when you choose. If you don't, we'll both question the decision."

She didn't get a chance to answer before there was a sharp knock on the door before it swung open abruptly. He wanted to curse, but he held it back as he looked over his shoulder. Standing there was Del, but right beside him was Addie March.

Fuck.

Chapter Sixteen

L ess than fifteen minutes later, the cots had been removed from her office, and Tamilya was dressed. Although, it didn't matter. The whole office probably knew they'd spent the night together. She knew there was already speculation about what was going on with them. She should probably be more upset, but with TFH, embarrassment was usual. In the FBI, it had been a threat to her career. Here they just bet on it.

She showed Addie into her office.

"So, you and Floyd are back together," Addie said, slight condemnation in her voice. Addie had never married, and she hadn't understood her relationship with Marcus back then. She definitely wouldn't understand it now, because Tamilya didn't really know what the hell was going on with it. At one time, Tamilya would jump to get her approval. Those days ended the moment she had let Tamilya take the blame for the Virginia Star bombing. Now, she didn't give a damn what the woman thought.

"Not really."

There was no indication that she was irritated, except for the way her mouth thinned.

Not much had changed in the last few years. Addie was still an imposing figure because of her size and her personality. Even though she was shorter than Tamilya, Addie constantly wore heels so she seemed taller. Tamilya had always thought she did it to give herself an edge over people. She may have been on a flight for eleven hours, but she looked perfect. Her hair was up in a tight twist at the nape of her neck, the severe look matched Addie's personality. The woman never allowed anyone to point out that Addie had made any flubs. The steel grey eyes still took in every bit of information the world would give her. Tamilya often thought Addie looked out at the world to find mistakes others made and somehow use that information against them. And she had wanted Tamilya to be just as cold-blooded as she was. Tamilya shivered. The thought that she would have ended up like Addie scared the bejesus out of her. Was that why she was holding back from Addie? She didn't take crap off anyone, and that was part of what appealed to Tamilya. She'd thought having such a tough mentor would be good. Tough and mercenary…that was a different story.

"I didn't know you were coming over here until TJ told me," Tamilya said. That bothered her, she didn't know why. It just did. No, she did know why. As the POC for the investigation, Addie should have told her she was coming. A text wasn't a hard thing. Hell, a fucking email would have sufficed.

"I was ordered to come over when all the connections were being made between the two incidents."

She raised her eyebrows. "So, the FBI is going to admit that I was right?"

Addie smiled. "Maybe you can get backpay for the years since?"

There was a tinge of sarcasm to her words, but Tamilya didn't know if it was for her or for the FBI. She was betting on both. Addie always saw herself as the injured party.

"Considering what I made while working for Conner Dillon, I really don't think that will be necessary."

Addie hesitated then nodded. "Alright, what do you have?"

"Not much and the FBI is really irritated that they have to read me in."

"Only one text so far?"

The memory of the taunt left an empty pit in her stomach. She knew she should want the bastard to text her because it would put them closer to catching him. Still, it left her feeling dirty. It stained her soul knowing that she hadn't been listened to all those years ago.

"Yeah. Just one text. Do you have anything in your memory that points to this? Any wording?"

She sighed. "I brought some files with me, and I thought maybe we could work together on them. For old time's sake?"

Addie wanted to know if Tamilya trusted her. With her career, that would be a big no. With the job, yeah, she would. At least for this investigation. She knew Addie would do anything to salvage her reputation that was growing more tattered by the minute. When Tamilya had been hired by Conner Dillon, the contract had included a clause allowing Dillon to fire her due to revelations about past cases. Seeing that he had wanted to hire her even after all the fallout from Virginia Star, Tamilya had been pretty safe. It was a different story for Addie. She still hadn't started her new position and, if the Virginia Star issue got messy again, it might threaten any jobs she had lined up. This was—once again—all about Addie.

Still, Addie had been with the FBI for over twenty years. Her brain and connections were what Tamilya needed here, so she would play nice for now.

"Yeah," she said, smiling. "Let's do this."

Addie smiled, relief filling her gaze. Maybe Tamilya had been reading the situation wrong.

"I didn't know you were retiring until you told me."

Addie pulled out her tablet and Bluetooth keyboard. "I just had enough. I got sick of seeing men moving forward, while the women kept having to fight for the small number of positions they would offer us. I could only take it for so long. And let's be honest, if you had been a man, they would have slapped you on the wrists and then let you go back to work. We will always be at a disadvantage."

"But you're going to work in the field?"

"Private company. Same thing, more money, better hours. What you used to have before you moved to TFH."

Tamilya sighed. "Yeah. Sadly, I missed the action. I got bored with working security measures for dignitaries and rich people."

Addie closed her eyes and sighed. "I can't wait."

When she opened her eyes, Tamilya felt the kinship they'd had between them. They had clicked immediately. They had nothing in common, other than their FBI background, and even that was different. But they both believed in the law. No black or white, just right or wrong.

"So, let's get started," Tamilya said.

"Yeah. The sooner we get done, the sooner I get to a beach."

"Planning some time in Hawaii?"

She nodded. "I haven't been here before, and I want to take a few days to spend on the island."

"I can't blame you. This place definitely gets in your blood."

MARCUS WAS SITTING in front Del remembering the time that he and his best friend Freddy had blown up the chemistry lab. They had snuck into the room to play with chemicals. Yeah, he had been a nerd. But what they hadn't expected was to make some miscalculations. Sitting in the principal's office and sitting in Del's office, felt the same. If his mother was nearby, he would worry she would appear and smack him upside the head again.

"So." Del said the word as he leaned back in his chair. Adam sat off to the side.

"You said a lot there, boss," Adam said with a smile.

"We need to know if this is going to affect your mission," Del said.

"No."

"Are you sure of that?"

Marcus nodded.

"And you thought it was a good idea to get it on in her office?" Adam asked. There was more humor than recrimination in his voice.

"We didn't do anything here. First, that's disrespectful to Tamilya and TFH. Second, she'd kick my ass if I tried. And third…"

He glanced up at the corner of the office and Del looked behind him. When he turned back around, understanding stamped his features.

"Yeah, good, because while I think anyone in TFH would only use it for betting purposes—and yeah, I know that is still going on—I would hate to think what would happen if it ever leaked."

Marcus held up his hands. "Promise. It would be damned near impossible to do anything on those cots."

"Desks work," Adam said. They both turned to him.

"Is that an observation or from experience?" Del asked.

Adam's mouth twitched. "Just a thought. No experience."

Del turned back to him. "But you thought you needed to sleep in there…"

"I was in front of her."

Understanding lit Del's eyes. "Protection. I doubt anyone would get in here."

"I do too, but I wasn't taking any chances. She gave me a little lip about it, because lord knows she's as good a shot as me."

"Better," Adam said.

"What?" he asked.

"She scored higher the last two months on the range." The smirk Adam was giving him was enough to irritate Marcus, but he didn't care. When it came to Tamilya, he didn't care if she out did him in everything.

"Damn. Okay, she's better, but I wanted them to have to go through me. I don't think they would want to kill her."

Adam and Del shared a look.

"What?" Del asked when he faced Marcus again.

He wasn't sure if he was being irrational or not, so he hesitated. "I think they may be after Tamilya. I'm worried that they wouldn't come here to kill her. I worry they would be coming to get her."

Again, his boss and second-in-command shared a look, then looked back at him. "Explain," Adam said.

"This is personal. The fact that they contacted Tamilya, that they picked Hawaii. Let's face it, Hawaii has some strategic value and, yes, we always remember Pearl Harbor on December seventh, but it would have little value to the mainland. The fear would be isolated. These people tend to want to make a big impact. The attack by the Japanese in '41 was strategic. Taking out our Pacific Command worked for the war. Doing a bunch of little bombs, or not so little, only goes so far. It will leave people on edge here and people on the mainland will change their vacations, but with a twenty-four-hour news cycle, they tend to forget.

Del sat back in his chair, the familiar squeak the only sound in the office.

"Have you talked to her about it?"

He shook his head. "I wasn't sure what I should tell her. I know she'll be pissed that I came to you first, and I couldn't really figure out why I thought she was a target. Tamilya likes facts not hunches. She might shoot me down and become entrenched. She might even push away protection because she wants to prove me wrong."

Adam sighed and rubbed the back of his neck. "That's probably true."

"What do you know about Addie?" Del asked.

"She's a bitch."

"Yeah, I agree. Anyone who leaves her people out to be blamed for something they should have handled makes them a bastard in my opinion. But now that she's here and up in our business, I need to know even more. Is there a chance that she would be looking to move ahead and use us in the process?"

Marcus shook his head. "She's leaving the FBI. Retiring. Tamilya said she'd lined up a security job with a big agency."

"Odd. What is she doing here?"

"Maybe she thinks she can help?" Adam suggested, then shook his head. "Okay, that doesn't sound right."

"I think she's worried it will hurt her at her new job. It will bring up all the scandal from that one fuck up and now she will have to explain herself."

Del nodded. "That sounds about right. She only does things for herself from what I have gotten out of Tamilya."

"Yeah, she had a rep in DC too," Marcus said.

Something caught Del's attention in the background, and he motioned with his hand. Marcus turned to see TJ in the office. He opened the door. "Did you need something from me?"

"Come in and shut the door. Addie March is already here."

He made a face and Marcus smiled. "So you feel the same way as I do."

TJ took the seat next to Marcus. "Don't get me wrong. The woman has a computer in her brain, but there was always this mercenary feel to her. Just be careful around her."

"She's retiring," Marcus said.

"I hadn't heard that, but we don't work for the same people. I don't blame her in a way."

"You think you would leave the FBI?" Adam asked, surprise in his tone.

He shook his head. "No, but if they try to transfer me, I will. Both Charity and I want to stay here."

"Thank God for that," Del said. Marcus couldn't hide his smile. No one would want to give up one of the best forensic scientists in the biz.

"But I've looked around and I've even talked to Dillon about a job. Definitely better pay, and March has a shit ton more experience than I do. She would get top dollar for her skills."

There was a knock at the door, and it was Charity. "Hey, seems there's a meeting of the minds in here."

"Do you need something?" Del asked.

"Yeah, we just had another text and I'm tracing it right now."

"Right," he said. "Get everyone in the common area. TJ, get hold of Smith and let him know we have another text."

"Already done. He's on his way in," Charity said with a smile. Then she shut the door and left them alone.

"Okay, so we have an asshole who definitely thinks he can mess with Tamilya," Del said, his voice threaded with anger. Marcus understood. She might have been with them for a short amount of time, but she was one of their own.

They walked out into the common room. The tables were always set in a u-shape. Cat, Drew, Autumn, and Graeme sat on the right side of the tables. Tamilya and Addie on the left. Marcus didn't hesitate. He walked over and took the seat next to Tamilya. She looked cool but Marcus knew better. He knew this was getting to her. Her hands were under the table and when he reached for one, he felt it fisted. He pried it open and took hold of her hand. She tightened her grip and he felt his nerves ease a bit. Not all the way, because for her to react that way, it had to be something horrible. He leaned closer to ask but Smith came rushing in.

"Hey, TJ, whatcha doing here?" he asked.

"I was dropping Charity off and stopped in to talk to Del when the text came in."

"Ah," he said, as he took the seat next to TJ, who was sitting next to Marcus.

Del was seated next to Charity. Adam stood in the background as Charity tapped on her tablet.

"This came in at seven oh five this morning."

The screen came to life and the words he saw chilled his blood. He had been right, even though he didn't want to be. This was more about Tamilya than anything else.

The minutes keep ticking and you keep running in circles. I will enjoy watching the life drain from your eyes when I kill you.

Chapter Seventeen

The moment Charity had told her what the text said, Tamilya knew what she had to do. There was one way to get this bastard, she needed to be the bait. It was the fastest way to get at the bomber. If he wanted her, she would throw herself out there like a big ass Neon sign.

Marcus was still holding her hand. He tugged on her their joined hands and leaned close enough to whisper.

"I know what you're thinking, and I have to object."

Dammit. Most women would love that a man knew them so well, but she didn't. Not right now. She was a target, which meant the hulking mass beside her could get hurt. She couldn't allow that. Not because of her.

She never wanted anyone to get hurt, but there were people in her life she would die to protect. Dead stop. Her family being at the very top of the list, and then there was Marcus. She turned and he was still close. The anger in his dark eyes would scare most women. Hell, it would scare most men. But not her. She knew what had to be done, and she would get Del to agree.

"Del, I need to talk to you," she said without taking her gaze from Marcus.

Their boss studied the two of them, then nodded. He rose from his seat.

"Cat, I want you to go back to the safe house. I know we have HPD there, but I want one of our own with the Lowes."

"Sure, boss."

"You're tracing it, yes?" he asked Charity.

"Yeah, but I'm expecting it to be a burner."

He nodded and then motioned to Tamilya. Marcus held onto her hand.

"Don't." It came out as a demand, but around the edges of it she heard the plea. He would never beg her, but she knew he was probably as close as he would ever get to doing just that.

She studied him. "What would you do if it were you?"

He didn't answer and he looked away for a second. When he finally looked at her again, irritation was easy to see in his expression. She watched his jaw flex, but he didn't answer. He didn't have to.

"Exactly."

She wiggled her hand away from his and hated the moment she stepped away from him. She instantly missed his heat. After drawing in a huge breath and releasing it, she squared her shoulders, and followed Del into his office, shutting the door behind her and taking one of the seats in front of his desk.

"You want to be bait?" Del asked.

Of course he knew. They all would do the same thing. They were a top-notch team, and she had no doubt, given time, they would find the perpetrator. The problem was that with each passing minute, another civilian could be put at risk.

"Yes. And I need Marcus working with someone else."

He cocked his head in question.

She sighed. "If they've been watching me, they know he and I are involved, somewhat."

What the hell they were she wasn't sure. He said he wanted more, but she couldn't even think about that right now. With an asshole threatening her, she couldn't contemplate the future.

"Yeah, I agree, but he's not going to be happy."

She snorted. "That is an understatement."

"He's giving us the death glare while TJ is trying to talk to him."

She turned in her seat to see Marcus doing just that. He didn't shy away because she knew he wanted to give her a message. He was going to fight this. As he kept his gaze locked with hers, he crossed his arms over his chest. After a moment, it was too much, and she turned back to Del.

"I'm not sure we have enough to go by to make you bait."

She nodded. That's what was bothering her. It would be easier to set a trap if she at least had an idea of any particulars. Information is what they needed, and background. They were flying blind and it wasn't a good position to be in.

"I'll have him working with Adam. You, I want here." She opened her mouth, but he held up his hand to stop her. "I get that you want to be out there, but the FBI is running down all the other leads. I want you here for the texts. You and Addie might be able to find something together. You two know the Virginia Star job better than any of us. Any texts might give us leads, but if you two are running around, we might miss out."

She frowned. "I would rather be out in the field."

He nodded. "I get that. I will make sure you are in on any bust. Promise."

Sighing, she nodded. There was a rap at the door, and it opened. She turned to see it was Adam.

"We traced the phone."

"That's not good," Del said.

She knew what he meant. It could be a trap of some sort. And she knew now she wouldn't be permitted to go on the bust. Anger moved through her fast and hard. This was her job and she wasn't going to be able to do it.

"Tamilya," Del said. She turned to face him. "I understand. I would want to be there, but this is one little bust and it could be a trap."

Outrage hit her at full force. "You just said I would be in on any bust."

"And this could just be a trap. I need you here waiting to see if there is another text."

"But…"

He stood up, his expression hardening. "I said I understand, but we need you here. There is every chance they are trying to draw you out there. We don't need that. We need you here safe and working with Addie and, to an extent, Charity."

She stood, trying to control her temper, but she felt it spiraling through her. She said nothing, but she nodded, acknowledging what he was saying. Adam stepped back and allowed her to pass. She knew he wanted to say something, but thankfully, he said nothing. As she tried to control her rage, she walked through the common area to her office. She knew without looking that Marcus had followed her. He shut the door.

"You aren't going."

She understood what he was saying. It wasn't that Del had told her no. Marcus was telling her that she would not be going—even if their boss hadn't just ordered her to stay at headquarters. Studying him, she saw he had already started preparing. He'd already pulled on his bulletproof vest and he had his side holster ready. All he needed was the helmet, but she knew he would wait until they got there for that. The fact that she wanted him even now as he stood there and ordered her to do something pushed her temper over the edge.

"You are saying I can't go?" She pronounced every word precisely. Her family knew to be wary of that tone. She didn't use it often because it took a lot to get her temper going. Keeping her from arresting the person who was threatening her was one thing that would do it.

"Yes. You need to stay here. Stay safe."

"If it had been you, would you do that? Would you stay here?"

He said nothing, but she read the expression on his face and knew his answer.

"Exactly. You would go."

"It's different."

"Because I'm a woman." She sighed, as the anger seemed to filter out of her. She was damned tired of fighting this fight. Of never being able to get people to take her seriously.

"No," he said.

Again she studied him as she crossed her arms beneath her breasts.

"So what is it?"

He opened his mouth, but there was a knock at the door seconds before it opened. Autumn popped her head in.

"Time to go, Hos," she said with a grin. It faded when she finally read the room. "Hurry up, Floyd. Boss said we have to get going before they move."

She left them, but also didn't close the door. They had no privacy in this damned place. What had she been thinking? Having a relationship with someone at TFH was stupid, but making all the same mistakes with Marcus… that was asinine.

"Just go."

He opened his mouth to argue with her, but she shook her head. "Go, because they will leave you."

"We'll talk when we get back."

"Do we really have anything to talk about?"

He nodded, never taking his gaze from hers. "We have a lot to discuss, but I won't be pushed into it when we both don't have time to talk."

"Just go," she repeated.

He hesitated, then he stepped forward, close enough so she could smell his scent. That sandalwood mixed with his own personal scent. It never failed to affect her. She thought he would grab her, but he brushed his mouth over hers, tenderly, softly…just enough to entice her. Then he stepped back.

"We *will* talk."

Then he was gone. She sat down in her chair and laid her head on her desk. She had made so many mistakes but trusting Marcus Floyd with her heart had to be the stupidest damned thing she had ever done. And she had done it twice. Two freaking times.

She could take a lot of things in her relationships, but

there were two at the top she couldn't. Cheating, which she knew Marcus would never do. The other was not respecting her. On any level, including work. She needed a man beside her who wouldn't keep her from succeeding and who had no problems with her career. She thought that was something she could expect from Marcus. But she had been wrong.

There was a knock at the door, and she looked up. It was Charity. "I just wanted to let you know that there were two more bombs found by the FBI."

She sat up. "What?"

"Two bombs. Little pipe bombs, but threats were sent in beforehand, so the FBI is handling it with HPD."

"Where?"

"Ala Moana park and then near the King Kame-hameha statue."

They were all really close to them, but she knew it had more to do with tourists. If the suspect could scare tourists and locals away from those spots, it would be detrimental to the economy. Ala Moana Center and Ward Center were hubs. Ward was a little ways away, but close enough that people would avoid it.

"No explosions?"

She shook her head. "I talked to one of the HPD techs. He said they think this had to do with the other bombing."

"Of course it did." Then she remembered the slip of paper they found in the hotel room.

"Ala Moana was on a list," she said mostly to herself. Her mind was jumping from one idea to the next but that one seemed to make the most sense. Ala Moana would be on a hit list and, if they were listing them in alphabetical order, that would be at the top of the list.

"No explosions. They're going with a theory that he was supposed to set up bombs all over Honolulu."

Jesus. That would make sense. The fear would send everyone into hiding. It would basically shut down Honolulu and Waikiki. Locals might just say screw it because, well, Hawaiians marched to their own tune. But tourists, now they would cower. The ones who were planning a trip would cancel it. Financially, this could devastate the islands. She'd heard stories about the weeks and months following 9-11. The beaches were bare except for locals and the military.

"Was the bomber ever identified?" she asked.

"Oh, didn't you hear?"

Tamilya shook her head.

"It was Wang Xiu."

She knew the name but, as usual, Charity filled in the blanks. "He worked for Li. Basically his favorite right hand man."

"Argh, seriously, is it the Chinese or is it the Russians? This is making my head hurt."

"I know, but agents are going over some things in the room he was staying in. HPD asked if I wanted to come over since the FBI said it was okay, so I am. I still have no idea why they didn't send the evidence here."

"Because of me."

"You?"

Tamilya nodded. "I'm a target right now and since we are starting to find the links to Virginia Star, they definitely don't want me near it."

"Ah. Okay. That's kind of stupid because I would guess you're an encyclopedia when it comes to that job."

Tamilya snorted.

"Well, I'll let you know if I find anything," Charity said, turning to leave and running into Addie.

"Oh, sorry, Agent March."

Addie gave her an understanding smile. "No worries, and call me Addie."

Charity returned the smile then hurried off.

"It's the right call," Addie said as she sat in the chair in front of Tamilya's desk.

"Shut up."

There was no heat in her words, but she didn't want to hear anyone tell her that she was wrong. She knew deep down in her gut that she should be at TFH. Charity was right, like she usually was. Tamilya and Addie would be considered the two people in the country who knew more about the Virginia Star bombing than anyone else. The two of them together would be able to remember facts that might not have made it into the final report. Anything, no matter how obscure, might be able to help them catch the bomber. Both she and Addie working together might be the best idea so far—even if she were still irritated at being left behind.

"Listen, let's look at the texts and see if we can find anything that matches them," Addie said. "I did get some analysis we can go over pointing to a male doing the texting."

"How so?"

"You know they have programs that can detect the sex of anyone based on their word patterns. I can go over them with you right now."

"Sounds good. Let's go out in the common area. It's so damned stuffy in the office, and that way we can spread out and use the big screen."

Addie nodded as they both rose and walked out of her

office. Everyone might be right, but she couldn't help feeling a little lost at the moment. Not because she thought she was right. If the roles were reversed, she would probably tell anyone else to stay.

This had to do with Marcus. If he would have said anything—just one word—of support, she probably wouldn't feel this way. She'd still be angry, but right now, she felt as if everything had ended in that one conversation. There was no going back to playing house after that. She had needed him to have her back, and he had left her hanging with no support. And because of that, she wasn't sure she could ever trust him again.

That was worse than having a terrorist threatening her.

Chapter Eighteen

Marcus was riding with Adam, who had the wheel. He couldn't concentrate on driving through the traffic, even though it was light. Midday on a weekday was nothing—especially after they found two unexploded bombs. The tourists were all hiding away in their hotels waiting for the all clear. None of them apparently thought that any high civilian area would be a target—including the hotels.

"Are you gonna to stop brooding and talk about it?"

He glanced at Adam. TJ was in one of the back seats ignoring them as he read his texts. His phone had been blowing up the entire ride thanks to the two bombs they had found. Everyone else had gone ahead, and they were speeding through the streets to catch up. Adam had waited for him.

"No."

"Well, then get your head out of your ass. Going in there like this will get you killed. Or worse, kill someone else. You don't want that on your hands."

Marcus grunted because he knew Adam was right, but it didn't change the fact that he felt Tamilya slipping away. It had never been a problem before. He could ignore his personal life and just work. That had always come first.

But now…he wanted Tamilya to come first. He had seen the look in her eyes when they'd been in her office. She'd accused him of not wanting her to go because she was a woman. He couldn't explain it then. It hadn't been that she was a woman, but that she was *his* woman. His world would be destroyed if she died. And while it was irrational and condescending, he had wanted her safe. He knew she could take care of herself, but with someone directly threatening her, he couldn't deal with it. And that was a mark against him.

"Uh," TJ said from the backseat.

"What?" Marcus asked, turning around.

"I decided that maybe I should check up on Addie and, well…she doesn't have any job waiting for her."

He frowned. "What are you talking about?"

"She isn't actually retiring with honors," he said looking down at his phone. "One of my buddies works in DC, and he said she was persona non grata. Seems she screwed up a few assignments, and they basically told her that she could retire but without any recommendations."

Marcus frowned. "She said she had several offers, but that she took the best one. Or that's what she told Tamilya."

"Then she was lying."

Adam's phone rang and he motioned with his head for Marcus to get it. It was Del.

"Hey, boss," he said.

"The FBI already went in. They found nothing, but

the phone. Oh, wait," he said. He heard someone shouting.

"Nothing?" Marcus asked. Del didn't answer right away.

"Well, fuck, they found Li in the house. Dead."

"Recently?" Marcus asked.

"Hold on," he said. Marcus ground his teeth even though he knew Del was getting information minute-by-minute.

"They're saying that he's cold, at least twelve hours."

He blinked. "He's been dead that long, which means his counterpart is on the island."

"Or, he or she was twelve hours ago," Adam said. He had since slowed down a bit and turned off the sirens.

"She. It's a woman, remember?" Marcus said, his mind trying to put all the pieces together and feeling as if he was missing one of them. That didn't happen around Tamilya because they always worked all of that out together. He hadn't realized how much he had come to rely on Tamilya talking him through a case until now.

"Uh, guys, we have a problem," TJ said from the backseat.

"What now?" Marcus growled.

"Addie March has been here longer than she said."

"What?"

"She arrived yesterday morning," he said.

"How do you know that?"

"Charity. She's with the HPD techs, and she did a little investigating. Addie was listed on the manifest of a plane coming the day before she said her flight got in."

In that one instant, everything clicked into place. Mother fucking Addie March.

"Turn around," he barked out. Adam glanced at him

but instead he addressed Del. "Boss, you need to head back to TFH. It's Addie March."

"Fuck," he said, not even questioning it. "We're on our way."

Adam turned on the sirens again and made a U-turn in the middle of an intersection. Marcus picked up his phone and started texting Tamilya.

Marcus: The bombers were involved with Addie. Be on your guard. We're on our way back.

He waited but she didn't respond. In fact, there wasn't a read receipt.

"I don't know why I didn't see it before," he muttered, praying that Tamilya would pick the phone up.

"What?" Adam asked.

"She's bitter. While she did everything to get ahead, it never happened. Granted, she made it pretty far up that ladder, but she could never break free of her past. The woman probably had something to do with Virginia Star bombing. I should have seen it."

She would have known all the particulars of the case. Tamilya had been taking her direction since Addie was the senior agent. And she had to be the one who steered Tamilya away from her hunches, leaving her to take the fall.

"How could you have known?" Adam asked.

"If Tamilya didn't pick up on it, how were you supposed to?" TJ asked, but he was double checking his weapons.

"I just should have. I never liked the woman, mainly because of her treatment of Tamilya, but there were other things. She had issues with anyone who wasn't under her thumb. She was a woman who always had to be in charge, and if not, she was sucking up to those in charge. If she didn't get her way, she would make sure the people responsible paid for it—one way or another."

"Did Tamilya answer?" Adam asked as he ran through a red light. Thankfully, it was late morning, so traffic had thinned out. Still, every mile felt like a thousand.

"No." And that heightened his worry. The idea that she could be hurt or in trouble or dead was unbearable.

He shook his head unable to form rationale words. Instead, he concentrated on them getting to TFH. He just prayed they were in time.

TAMILYA LEANED back in her chair and tried to think but it wasn't easy. She knew the team was with the FBI and she wanted to be there. Needed to be there. But she was stuck here doing stupid research.

"You're being a little immature about this. You know in your heart that this is the best way to proceed."

Addie's voice was starting to grate on her nerves. Tamilya was wondering if she hadn't been blamed for the Virginia Star bombing, how long she would have stuck it out working for Addie. With a few years distance, she could see what she'd missed before. Instead of being about finding the truth, Addie had always been about what could get her ahead. Even now, she was here, and not because Tamilya needed her. Nope, she was here because of her post-FBI career. She had to be one of the most self-centered agents Tamilya had ever met.

They had started out in the conference area, but moved back to her office. Tamilya just couldn't think out there and decided to move back. Nothing was coming to her though.

"So, have you decided on where to go after you retire?" she asked, needing a diversion. Anything but thinking about what she was missing out on. She glanced at her phone waiting, waiting…waiting. But nothing came. She assumed that Marcus would tap her in, but she wasn't sure how much control they had over that. With Agent Smith in charge of things like this, there was a good chance only Del was allowed on coms. It was stupid and territorial, but when the FBI got involved, they liked to take over.

"Nope. I have a few offers. I'm thinking maybe Miami. Kind of sick of the DC winters."

She smiled. "I don't blame you. I didn't realize how conditioned I was to the cold weather until I was here my first year. All of a sudden, I realized it was December and I was sitting by my parents' pool."

"They doing okay?"

She nodded. "Since Dad retired, his health has improved, and Mom loves Hawaii."

"That's good. Kind of a dream to retire to Hawaii and just hang out."

"You would never be able to do that," Tamilya said.

Addie smiled. "Yeah. But neither could you."

She wasn't so sure of that. The drive to be the best TFH agent she could be rode on her back, but she didn't want to do it forever. While she was proud of her work since she started at TFH, she didn't want to do it until she died. On the other hand, Addie would probably be at work until the day she died.

"I'm going to grab myself a cup of coffee," Addie said breaking into Tamilya's thoughts.

She nodded but said nothing else.

"Do you want any?"

Tamilya blinked and looked up at her old boss. In all their time working together, Addie had never offered to get her anything.

"Uh, no thanks. Don't need to add caffeine to the situation."

She smiled and slipped from the room.

Tamilya leaned back in her chair, her foot tapping on the floor. She couldn't stop fidgeting as anxiety rode her hard. She wasn't just pissed at the moment. In fact, some of her anger had bled out of her. She wanted to be out there, wanted to take the bastard down, but Del had been right. She would have been a distraction to the other officers.

She stood and started to pace her office. There wasn't much room, but there was enough for her to use it to think. It wasn't just that she could be there to take down the bastard. Her team was there. She wanted to back them up, be by their sides.

She stopped pacing and closed her eyes. If anything happened to any of them, she would be so upset, but if anything happened to Marcus…

Opening her eyes, she pushed that thought aside. She didn't want to even contemplate that. Just like a lot of other law enforcement, she was a tad bit superstitious. Thinking it could make it a self-fulfilling prophecy. Instead, it would be better to concentrate on the case.

With another Li associate gone, was he the one involved with the whole thing? Had he been working with the Russians four years ago? The countries were known to work together against the US every now and then. Their location and dictatorships made it easy to think they would want to do anything to Western democracies.

Her phone vibrated on her desk and she stepped closer to grab it, but Addie stopped her.

"Don't," she said.

Tamilya looked up and saw that Addie was holding a gun on her. That irritated Tamilya, but it was the pipe bomb she held in her other hand that turned Tamilya's blood to ice.

Chapter Nineteen

The smile curving Addie's mouth held no humor. There was a satisfaction, but Tamilya couldn't see a shred of a remnant of the woman she had known four years ago. The chill she'd felt in her bones, now seeped into her blood...even her soul. Was she ever the woman Tamilya thought she was?

"Your expression is priceless, really." She let out a tinkle of a laugh that heightened Tamilya's fear, but she would be damned if she would show it.

"Why?"

She shrugged and the smile turned smug. "Why not?"

Tamilya blinked. The tone was one she had never heard before. At least not coming from Addie. She had always been the perfect agent, the type they would talk about in their recruiting literature and videos. Now, bitterness dripped from every word, along with a sing song quality that left Tamilya's stomach queasy.

How had she missed this side of Addie?

Addie sighed. "Fine. I'll tell you. Sit down."

Tamilya hesitated, but Addie waved her gun.

"I can make it so you have to sit down. A bullet to the knee is very painful."

She hated to do it, because it put her at a disadvantage. She was already shorter than Addie, but Tamilya knew sitting behind the desk would trap her. Still, she didn't see a way out of it.

She sat.

"What a good little agent," she said, the resentment in her voice growing more prominent with each word she said. "Let me tell you a little story. See, there was a girl who grew up with a father in the FBI."

Great, now she was treating her like a child. Tamilya didn't need a damned story. What she needed was the truth. She doubted she would get that from Addie. Tamilya had known Addie had kind of a warped view of how the FBI should work for her. As a legacy, she felt she should get special treatment. But Tamilya had no idea she was this bent.

"And when she graduated at the top of her class at Columbia, she decided to go into the FBI. Being a lawyer seemed so fucking boring. So, she went to Quantico and, once again, she graduated at the top of her class. Actually, I was number five. That was a feat for a man, but damned near impossible for a woman. You think you had it bad? Try being in a class that only had three other women, two of whom dropped out because of the bullying."

Tamilya knew she needed to find common ground. They both had suffered because of the patriarchy in law enforcement.

She opened her mouth, but Addie stopped her by waving the gun.

"My story," she muttered, sounding like a toddler who hadn't had her nap. Only, she was a toddler holding a gun who wanted to kill anyone in her way. Mainly Tamilya. She could care less who got hurt in the process.

"I was just going to ask if you could put the bomb down."

Addie looked down at her hand as if she had forgotten it was there. "No. I think I'll hold onto it." She raised her head and locked her gaze on Tamilya's. The woman was bonkers, but she was deadly and damned smart. She knew showing Addie any fear would only get her off. She just hoped she masked the panic rising up in her right now.

"Now, where was I?"

"Bullying?"

"Ah, yes. There were threats, verbal and physical."

That part of the story was definitely true. Tamilya knew from her own experience it wasn't easy for a woman, but Addie went through the program twenty years earlier.

"Did you report it?"

She rolled her eyes. "No. I knew that nothing was going to happen. We both know that at that time, reporting abuse of that sort would ruin my career. Besides, I talked to my father about it."

Addie's father and grandfather had both worked for the FBI. Tamilya had heard the stories of their bravery, but she had also heard the whispers about Addie's father. He had been a bastard of a supervisor against anyone at the Bureau who wasn't white…and male.

"Yeah, I can see you know how that went. My father told me to stop being a lazy whore and earn my way into the FBI just like the men. From that moment on, I knew I was by myself."

Addie had no sisters or brothers, so she had been his only child. He had left her to be abused and attacked because of her sex. Being his daughter would make her more of a target too.

"And you did well."

She snorted. "Are you kidding me? If I were a man, I would be higher up in the organization."

Tamilya doubted that. Addie had been mercenary in her work, and she had definitely gotten on the bad side of those in charge. At the time Tamilya had worked for her, she hadn't seen it. Or maybe, she just saw it as both of them against the others. They were the ones left out to dry over the Virginia Star bombing. But Tamilya had never been someone to knock heads. She had worked with others, made her way through the ranks until she landed in Addie's division.

"Once I started working, not much changed. I had a few bosses here and there that were decent, but for the most part, they were a bunch of bastards."

Tamilya nodded as if understanding. There was a good chance that Addie was telling the truth. There was also a chance that she was clinically insane, so everything was distorted. If she kept her talking, there might be a way she could gain access to her desk drawer where she locked her weapon. The key was in her front right pocket. She just needed to keep Addie talking.

"They didn't see the value of my hard work. Do you know how long it took me to get to head the terrorism division?"

"Twenty years."

She snorted. "Of course, you did know that. Twenty years! I had fellow classmates who had fucked up on the job and got ahead faster. All because they were men."

Again, Tamilya nodded because she was sure it was true. There were still issues on every level of law enforcement when it came to women. Back then it didn't matter how good a woman was, it was next to impossible to get ahead. A woman could be the best agent in the group, but thanks to her vagina, she would be passed over.

"And then there was you."

Tamilya blinked at the venom in Addie's voice. "What?"

"You showed up and everyone went on and on about you. That you were some kind of fantastic brainiac."

Great, so doing her job had ended her up in this place. It was just her luck that she was smart enough to get ahead at work but too stupid to see the traitor right in front of her.

"It was irritating, but not as irritating as when you discovered the cell for the Virginia Star bombing. Do you know how long I had been planning that?"

Her head started to pound as her anxiety rose to another level. As Addie had started ranting about everything, Tamilya had realized that she had been tangled up with the bombing. She had never thought she actually planned it.

"It was about the time they passed me over for Agent in Charge. I had the qualifications. I knew the job, did my work, but then, they promoted Kent Lautner."

She spit the name out, and Tamilya agreed with the feeling. Two years after being appointed, Lautner had been suspended, then fired and prosecuted for sexual assault of a fourteen-year-old girl.

"Did he assault you?"

She shook her head. "No. I wasn't in his age range apparently." She shivered as if disgusted by it. "But I knew he was slime. I didn't know he was that bad, but from what I read later, he had a taste for the young innocent ones. That is something you cannot call me. So, there I was, working my ass off, trying to protect America, and they gave me nothing. Worse, they put a bastard in the job that I should have had."

Tamilya knew the story, had heard it whispered. But she had heard other whispers that she chose to ignore at the time. Addie had a temper and she tore down anyone who got in her way. You can't rise up in the ranks if you are stabbing people in the back left and right.

"So, two years before the bombing?" Tamilya asked.

"Yes. Two years. I knew all the players, knew they wanted to do something on US soil, so I offered up my services."

"How much?"

Addie blinked. "What?"

"How much did they pay you?"

"I didn't do it for the money," she spat out, seemingly disgusted with the idea.

"You didn't do it for free."

She smiled. "No. There were a few million reasons to be compensated. And when it went off and the FBI played the fool by saying they had caught the bomber and all was well, I was treated like a queen."

And Tamilya's career had been in tatters in what someone might call a twofer. "But why now? Why come to Hawaii?"

"There's been others, you know." The tone she used made her sound like a little girl sharing a secret.

"What?"

"Others. The USS Franklin, the embassy in Columbia. I helped with all of them."

She blinked realizing that Addie wasn't just a danger,

she might really be insane. She sounded so damned proud of herself.

"And now Hawaii. Why Blaisdell?"

She rolled her eyes. "That was supposed to be here."

"Here?" she asked, her blood icing completely over. "Task Force Hawaii?"

She nodded, a secret smile playing about her mouth. "You were going to be my triumph."

"And who was paying for that?"

She waved her gun. "Several sources. Chinese and Russian. They really don't like the US." She said the last sentence as if she were revealing some great secret.

"And why TFH?"

She shrugged. "They just wanted to create some havoc, and I talked them into Hawaii. They're so damned stupid."

"Because Hawaii is isolated."

"Right? They just didn't see that while the mainland would be upset, they wouldn't be affected like a bombing campaign say in the Midwest."

"So why did you come here?"

Again she rolled her eyes. "You. You ruined everything."

It was Tamilya's turn to blink. "What?"

"You had people talking in the FBI. They were reviewing old cases."

Tamilya opened her mouth to ask her more questions.

"That's it. That's all I owe you."

"So, you're going to die after all of this."

"What?"

"You have a pipe bomb. You're—"

"What in this story makes you think I'm going to kill myself? I am *not* a fucking martyr. I would have died for my country at one time, but they lost that loyalty long ago. No, this has a trigger. First, I shoot you, then I leave the bomb. By the time they realize I'm not here, I'll be somewhere extradition is impossible, living with my millions."

Sadly that was true. She could kill Tamilya and run away. It would be at least a day before they realized she was the only one there and Addie was off running around with her millions as she said. She had finally worked the key to her drawer out of her pocket, but she would have to bend down to unlock the drawer.

"Why are you waiting? Why don't you just shoot me and be done with it?"

* * *

Marcus tried his best to cool his fear, the outright panic that now coursed through every cell of his body. They were just a couple minutes from TFH, but he knew that every minute meant that she could be lying there dead. Or worse, taken to another location.

He looked down at his phone. Still no answer.

"Anything?" TJ asked.

He shook his head.

No one spoke, but they heard the calls from other divisions. HPD and FBI were coming to help, but he knew they had the best chance.

Adam turned into the parking lot at break neck speed, crashing through the gate. He came to a screeching halt as they all hurried out of the car. His heart was in his throat, each beat seemingly blaming him for not seeing this. There had always been rumors about the woman, but now, it seemed that she was ready to throw it all out. What she gained out of this, he had no idea, and he didn't give a fuck. What he cared about was saving Tamilya. He had never told her he loved her. He wanted her, needed her on a level that embarrassed him, but he had known for a while that he loved her. The way she smiled at him…or frowned. Shit, all she had to do was be breathing.

He was about to burst into the building, but Adam held him back.

"Get your hands off me, man," he growled.

"Wait, we need to assess the situation. If we run in there without thought, we could get her killed."

Marcus hated that Adam was right. He gave him a nod.

"Silence on the coms, hand signals," Adam said. Then he looked at Marcus. "Maybe you should stay out here."

He shook his head. "No way."

"It's the same reason we kept her here…"

Then his voice trailed off. "Which was a set up to get her alone. Addie has it out for her."

"Okay, but we need to be extra careful. Explosives are all through this case. Who knows what that bitch has?"

TJ chuckled. "Bad words from Adam. It's bad."

"Remember, hand signals. No talking."

He heard others start to show up, and he barely glanced back at them. But he saw Del running toward them and HPD SWAT screeching to a halt. They were first on the scene and since it was their headquarters, they didn't wait.

They made their way into the building, their backs against the wall as they all worked in tandem. He knew that until they had a reason, no one else would be called in. That was standard operation procedure.

As they filtered into the office, they noticed that Tamilya's door was open and they heard voices. Adam gestured with his head but held up his hand to wait. As he held his back against the wall, Adam inched closer to the office as TJ and Marcus stayed in their positions. Seconds ticked by and finally he motioned for them to come closer. With every little inch, Addie and Tamilya's voices grow louder.

Then he heard the words that stopped his heart in its tracks.

"Why don't you just shoot me and be done with it?"

Red haze and terror clouded his vision. He had his head on before, but right now, Tamilya just asked to be shot. Just like that. She thought she was alone, and she was willing to just give up and let Addie shoot her. All his worst fears rushed through him, leaving only anger in its place. He wasn't willing to let her go, to give her up. He had only just found her again, and he wasn't able to contemplate being without her.

He rushed forward knowing that it went against all of his training. It's always better to take it slow, to make sure you know where the primaries are before you rush in, but his head wasn't working. Only his heart…and his soul. If he lost her now, he would never recover. He knew that.

He stopped short of the door listening.

"Don't worry. It won't hurt. I couldn't just leave you with a bomb because I wouldn't be one hundred percent sure you would die. You never know how that is going to end up."

Marcus moved just a little closer and that's when he saw Tamilya. She was sitting at her desk, looking over it as if that was where Addie was. There was a good chance she was there because the office was small. He must have made a move because he sensed Tamilya knew he was there. She lowered her head and looked out of the side of her eye. Her gaze connected with his, and she shook her head as if telling him to wait.

Then she raised her head. "You think that bomb won't go off when you set it down?" she asked, letting him know there was a bomb with some kind of a trigger. Probably more of an IED kind of device, which worked well with pipe bombs.

"I don't, but I'm pretty sure of it," Addie said, he couldn't tell where she was. "The remote won't work on it until I connect a few wires."

That's all he needed to know. He figured out where Addie was by where her voice had come from. If he rushed fast enough, he would definitely be able to at least gain the upper hand.

Without hesitation, he rushed forward, kicking the door open. He hadn't thought her stupid enough to stand right behind the door, but she was close enough that it clipped her. Addie let loose a howl that sounded like a banshee, screeching profanities at him as she turned the gun toward him.

"You fucking bastard," she yelled. He knew the best way to deal with her was to rush her. Closing the distance would throw her aim off.

He felt the heat of a bullet hit his right shoulder, but he ignored it. Adrenaline was pumping so fast through him that he barely felt it. They went falling onto the floor, Addie hit her head on the chair before landing with a thud beneath him. He held her down, but she wasn't moving. He looked down and found her eyes closed. He felt for a pulse and found it easily. She had dropped the bomb and that had him pulling himself off the ground and looking for Tamilya. She was right there and he didn't wait. He grabbed her.

"What?" she yelled as he shoved her through the doorway and slammed the door shut without explaining.

He didn't answer her. Instead, he kept running, pushing her through the office. He yelled, "Bomb, take cover."

Everyone scattered at that point and he realized there were more people in area. The rest of the team was there. They all hurried outside, running away from the building. He wrapped his arms around Tamilya and watched the building. She kept trying to say something, but he ignored her as he waited. Seconds ticked by and her muffled curses got louder. Finally, he loosened his hold.

"What?"

"She said that she hadn't connected all the wires."

"If there's explosives, you can't mess with that. You never know what is going to happen."

He looked over to see Sgt Kalama, the head of the EOD division of HPD SWAT. Then he heard the beeping behind him and watched as the bomb robot was wheeled down the pathway.

"Addie's in there," Tamilya said. "We should get her out of there."

He kept his arms tightly around her. For some reason, he felt if he let her go, he might collapse.

"Fuck Addie."

She snorted. "I agree, but she will have a lot of information about the networks she used."

He turned, releasing his hold for just a second. Then he cupped her face. "The woman wanted to kill you."

"I know."

"She shouldn't be allowed to live."

"Believe me, I understand that. But I also want the information she has. We could save so many more lives."

"They'll get her out of there."

"I know. I just want to make sure we get her alive so

we can get that information. She had connections to both the Russians and Chinese and who knows what else."

He opened his mouth to argue, but the world around him started to spin. His stomach roiled. It was then he realized there was blood on his hands. He'd gotten some on Tamilya's face. Was that her blood? He looked her over as his vision started to fade.

"Marcus?" she asked, worried. "What's wrong?"

"You know I love you."

He never heard her response because he started falling toward her and his world went black.

Chapter Twenty

Tamilya paced the waiting room anxious to hear about Marcus. Her nerves were beyond raw. Every time someone came in the waiting room, her heart jumped into her throat. She just kept walking around, because when she sat down, her emotions tied her in knots.

"You should get checked out," Del said.

She cut him a look but kept on pacing. They had been diverted to Tripler Army Medical Center as Queen's had been handling a three-car crash. She had been irritated, and she still was. He was a damned hero and he had to go to another hospital?

"I did get checked out. Doc said everything was okay."

She didn't stop or even slow down to answer. She had to keep moving.

You know I love you.

Those whispered words had warmed her heart, but he had said them as he was passing out. Was he in his right mind? Right now, she didn't care. She just wanted to see him. Even if he said he didn't mean the words now, she didn't care. She just wanted him to be okay.

Del grunted. When Tamilya glanced at him, he was looking down at his phone.

"What?" she asked as she kept pacing.

"March is okay. She has a world class concussion."

"Good."

This was Addie's fault. Everything. From the bombings to Marcus. Addie had been after her, not anyone else. Oh, she wanted the money, but she had come after Tamilya because of the hatred she felt for her. Tamilya didn't know how she had missed it, especially after what Addie had done to her after the Virginia Star bombing. That should have been the first sign that there was something seriously wrong with her relationship with Addie. She couldn't call it a friendship because they had never been friends. It was all her fault that people had been hurt. That Marcus had been shot.

"Stop blaming yourself."

She tossed Del a look. Everyone else was still clearing things up. The FBI had Addie in custody, and they would handle it from this point on. Both she and Marcus would be called as witnesses, but thankfully, they wouldn't have to be involved otherwise.

"I know what you're going through."

"Really?" She couldn't keep the sarcasm out of her voice.

"You know how Emma and I met?"

She stopped and looked at him. "It was that serial killer case, right?"

He nodded. "I missed the signs, didn't take enough precautions. She almost died because I missed the signs. I was more at fault than you'll ever be."

Tamilya started pacing again. "You should just let me be then."

No matter what he said, she knew Marcus was hurt because of her. She wasn't to blame for that crazy bitch and her plot. But the fact that Addie had focused on Tamilya had put him at risk. And all of her TFH Ohana too.

"Tamilya," he said, trying to calm her again. It would do no good. Fear, recrimination, and a healthy dose of rage still bubbled beneath her surface. With a sigh, he scrubbed his hand over his face as Emma came blowing through the double doors, her face filled with worry and indignation. Tamilya stopped as she watched her rush over the Del. He hadn't even been in danger, but Tamilya could see the terror Emma felt. It was the same feeling she had in the pit of her stomach when she heard the gun go off.

Emma launched herself at Del, who easily grabbed her. He whispered something to her that Tamilya couldn't hear before he set Emma on the ground.

She looked at Tamilya. She knew that Emma wasn't good with touching other people, and they didn't know each other well. So when Tamilya found herself pulled into a hug, she blinked and looked at the boss. He was looking at the two of them with a warm smile.

Emma stepped back, but she kept her hands on Tamilya's upper arms. She towered over Emma but the strength she saw comforted Tamilya. This was one woman she would not want to mess with.

"He will be all right. He's a fighter."

Tamilya sighed. "He lost a lot of blood."

She tsked. "He'll make it."

Tamilya felt the backs of her eyes burning and had to

blink back tears. She hadn't been able to think since Marcus had pitched forward in a faint. The paramedics had reassured her over and over that he'd lost some blood, but he would be fine. She wouldn't believe that he was okay until she saw him. She needed to see him. Then, she would know for sure.

"You need evidence," Emma said nodding. "I understand. But I promise you, from what Del told me, the chances of him dying are very slim."

Just hearing the words *chances* and *dying* had panic setting in again.

"Emma," Del said, aggravation riding through his tone.

She released Tamilya and looked back at her husband. "What? I'm just giving her information. She will do better with facts. Oh, look, your parents and Cat are here."

That's when she noticed her mother rushing towards her, her father close behind. Cat took her time strolling in behind them.

"My baby," her mother cried as she pulled her into a hug.

It was those tortured words from her mother, and the fear she saw in her father's eyes, that caused her to finally break down. Tears filled her eyes as she shivered, the day's events hitting her. Addie's deception, the fact Marcus had risked his life for hers.

You know I love you?

Oh, God, why did she think she didn't love him? That this was just for fun, that she could keep her heart uninvolved? It hadn't worked last time. This time, it was so much worse. Why had she wasted their time together and not taken a chance? She could have lost it all today. Lost him.

Her mother let her go so that her father could hug her. Feeling his strong arms surround her gave her comfort, but she couldn't stop crying. Not when she might have lost a chance to tell Marcus that she loved him. Still.

"Ms. Lowe," someone called out. She turned to find a nurse standing at the entrance to the surgery area. She hurried forward.

"You're Ms. Lowe?"

She nodded.

Relief softened the older woman's features. "Good, because I wouldn't want to go in there again without you."

Tamilya blinked. "What?"

"Agent Floyd is throwing a fit. He's refusing to have anything but a local until he sees you."

"Does he need more than a local?"

"No, but he's so agitated, it's causing issues. We need you back there."

She nodded and turned to look back at everyone who had gathered there. "I'll be right back."

Then she followed the nurse. They walked down a long hallway until stopping in front of a door. "You need to clean up."

"Clean up?"

"Yeah, you have blood—I'm assuming Agent Floyd's —on your face. He might be upset if he sees it."

She nodded and stepped into the bathroom. When she saw herself in the mirror, her eyes filled up again. She was trying not to get too excited. Until she saw him, she wouldn't believe he was safe.

She hurried and cleaned up her face, then stepped back out of the bathroom.

"Good," the nurse said with a smile. "This way, Ms. Lowe."

"It's actually Agent Lowe."

"Oh, I'm sorry. He didn't convey that when he told me to fucking go find Tamilya Lowe."

Tamilya swallowed a laugh but it bubbled up into a sob.

"Oh, sweetie," she said, stopping so she could wrap her arms around Tamilya. "Everything is going to be okay. He's just being a pain the ass like all men are when they are hurting."

She drew in a deep breath and nodded. "Thank you."

"Now, he's going to be stitched up, and it was a through and through. No bones involved. Minimal damage or he would be dead by now since he's refusing to be stitched up. It's just that he lost some blood and the stress of the situation sort of pushed his wound to be more critical."

"But you're going to put him out? You said a local would work."

"On most people but with his emotional state right now, we're worried about working on him like that. Doc wants to put him under so that we don't have to deal with him." She shook her head. "Men."

As if to prove her point, Marcus bellowed, "I said no. Not until my Tamilya is here."

His words were slurred, but they were the most beautiful sound in the world to her.

Drawing in another deep breath, she released it, and straightened her shoulders. With a nod to the nurse, she went into the room.

"Marcus Floyd, what the hell do you think you're doing?"

He was laying on his back. His shirt was gone, and he

had a blanket draped over him. The operating room was filled with people and equipment.

A doctor pulled down his face mask. "Please tell me you're Tamilya."

She nodded.

"Tamilya, woman, get over here."

She almost moved over there, but she stopped herself.

"I think you need to check that tone, Floyd."

He chuckled. "Yep, that's her. Come here. *Please*."

She did as he asked and went to his side. His eyes were barely opened.

"Drugged?" she asked the doctor.

He nodded. "We're worried because he's refused to go completely under. I know he's a big guy but, we didn't want to give him any more."

She nodded, then leaned down so Marcus could see her.

"Marcus, you need to quit being a big baby and have the wound stitched up."

"Not being a baby. They wouldn't tell me anything." It was almost adorable that he was pouting.

"We told you she was fine," the doctor said with irritation.

"Don't trust you," he said, his gaze drooping more. "Had to make sure you were okay, Tammy."

"I am. Sitting out in the waiting room with everyone else."

"Okay. Love you."

Then before he could go completely under, she said the words she had failed to use earlier. "I love you too, you idiot. Now do what the doctor says."

But the words were wasted, he was already under. She

rose up and the doctor was already pulling his mask back up.

"Thank you."

She nodded. "Just make sure you take good care of him."

Then she walked out the door and back down the hall to where everyone else was waiting. Del was off to the side on the phone, but everyone else had gathered together. The only one missing now was Adam, but since he was their POC for HPD, she had a feeling he was busy with them.

"He's going to be okay," she said. "They're starting on him right now. It was a through and through."

There was a collective sigh of relief as her mother came to put her arm around Tamilya.

Del came walking forward and held out his phone. "She wants to talk to you."

"Who?"

"Just take it."

She took the phone and held it up to her ear.

"Hello," a woman said on the other end.

"This is Agent Lowe."

"Oh, good. This is Ashley Floyd."

She blinked and then narrowed her eyes at a smiling Del. She was going to kill her boss. He just threw her to Marcus' mother without a thought.

"I understand you got to see Marcus."

"Yes, he's doing fine. The wound is a through and through." Then she realized his mother might not know what that meant. "It's when—"

"I know what it is," she said cutting off Tamilya. "I'm going to be on a plane here in about an hour. Del said he's going to pick me up, but that you were staying with Marcus."

Her anger rose and she started contemplating on how to kill Del. She knew she could hide the body. The only problem wouldn't be fooling the authorities, but Emma. She would definitely know Tamilya was involved once she heard what Del had done.

"I was for my protection and because of the case."

There was a long pause. "You're telling me I have to stay at a hotel?"

"No. No, I'll probably move back home."

"Why?"

"Why what?'

"Why are you moving home? Listen, I know my boy and I know he wouldn't have demanded to see you if you were just friends. He's been pining away after you for months now."

"He told you?"

"Not your name, but a mother knows. He's been hiding something from me, and I knew he was tangled up about a woman."

She didn't know what to say to that.

"So, again, do I need a hotel room?"

She cleared her throat and drifted away from her folks. "No."

"Good. I'm about to be dropped off at the airport. Del will be picking me up, so I will see you then."

The phone went dead. Del held out his hand with a smirk on his face. She handed him the phone, then leaned in to whisper. "I'm going to pay you back."

"I don't doubt it, but believe me, it's better than waiting. You have it all settled and things can move forward."

"You think you're so smart," she said, not wanting to admit he had been right.

"Nope, I just know people and I know mamas," he said nodding in the direction of her parents. She took the hint.

She smiled at her parents as she walked over to them, getting another hug. "You guys probably want to go home."

"No. We're waiting," her mother said sitting back down. Her father joined her.

"But you've been at a safe house for a couple days. I thought for sure you would want to be at the house."

"And we can wait a little bit longer to find out about Marcus," her mother said. The tone she used told Tamilya that her mother wasn't going to budge.

"Besides," her father said conversationally, "I think I need to have a chat with the boy when he wakes up."

Leave it up to her father to equate a 250-pound mountain of man meat with a boy. She understood when Ashley did it. She was his mother and would always see him as a little boy. Her father was another story.

Her mother took Tamilya's hand. "We want to wait. This is important to your team."

It warmed her heart to know that her mother got it. Tamilya had a solid base with her own family, but more than any other team she had worked with, she fit with TFH. They always saw her as one of their own. They were kind of an oddball group, but they were hers.

She nodded and sat down. There were low murmurs throughout the room, all the couples talking amongst themselves. Autumn plopped down beside her.

"So, wanna talk about it?"

"Not really."

"I bet you won't give me a date." Autumn's voice was filled with irritation.

Tamilya looked at her friend, then narrowed her eyes as Autumn pretended interest in her fingers.

"This is about the bet."

She gasped, her eyes widening. The reaction was so overblown, she had to fight a laugh. "You think I want deets about your sex life because of the bet?"

Tamilya let one eyebrow rise and waited.

"Okay, that's part of it," Autumn said with a laugh. "The other part is that I'm your friend."

"And?"

"And I need to live vicariously through you because I haven't had a man in my bed for a really long time."

Tamilya knew that wasn't *exactly* true, but she let it slide. "As a friend, I can tell you that Addie is lucky she only has a concussion and is in FBI custody."

"Why?"

"If not, I would have beat the crap out of that bitch."

For a moment, Autumn said nothing as she studied her, then she threw her head back and laughed. The sound bounced off the walls drawing attention from everyone else. Before she had to explain anything, a young man stepped into the waiting room, carrying a huge box.

"Hey, cuz," Drew said as he approached the man. "I see Auntie Marlene got my text."

The other man nodded. "Any news?"

"All looks good. They're just sewing him up."

Cat stepped up to her husband as he set the box on one of the chairs.

"Time to eat," she said to the room. And as always, everyone from TFH didn't hesitate.

Her mom looked at Tamilya. "You should eat."

She shook her head. If she had a bite to eat before she heard Marcus was totally in the clear, she might just throw up.

"Maybe in a little bit," she said, and her mother smiled.

"Hey, the Lowes should eat first, you heathens," Del said as the team descended on the food like locusts.

She smiled. Yep, they were a part of her family. Crazy and a little dysfunctional, but definitely part of her family. The thought warmed her heart, and she used it to calm her nerves while she waited.

MARCUS CAME AWAKE SLOWLY. The sound of machines beeping filled the room and the clean antiseptic smell of the hospital hit him. He took stock of his body. His shoulder ached, but not too badly. More than likely, it would as soon as the meds from surgery wore off.

He tried to move his hand but found it impossible. He turned to look and saw someone was holding it. There was just enough light in the room to see that Tamilya was sitting by his side. Her head was laying on the bed, as she held his hand in a death grip.

He had fuzzy memories of the night before, but most of them involved laying on the table waiting for surgery and refusing to have it done unless he spoke to Tamilya. His gaze traced over her features. She was safe, that was all that mattered.

Marcus knew he should let her rest, but he was a selfish man. Especially after yesterday. The fact that he realized he'd wasted over four years without Tamilya, and he could have lost her...his hand twitched. That little movement had her head popping up off the mattress. Her eyes were still hazy with sleep, and even in the darkened room, he could see the stress had taken its toll on her these last twenty-four hours.

"Hey," she said, a smile curving her lips.

In that one moment, he wanted to tell her everything. He knew that he had told her he loved her. What he didn't know was if she loved him. Sure, he had forced her to say it in the operating room, but he wasn't sure if she didn't say it just to appease him.

"Hey yourself," he said and mentally rolled his eyes. Clever, Marcus, really clever.

"Del just stepped out to take a call, but he'll be back."

"I don't care about him. Just you," he said, raising their joined hands so he could brush his mouth over her fingers. "I seem to remember forcing you to tell me that you loved me."

She shook her head, suddenly acting shy.

"I remember that part. Don't lie."

"What I meant was that you didn't force me. I do love you."

His heart jolted at those four words. "Yeah?"

She nodded, a smile curving her lips.

"We have a lot to talk about," he said.

"I agree, but Del is about to come back in here."

And the rest of the TFH Ohana would show up. There were rules about how many visitors a person could have in their room, but they tended to ignore that.

"And your mother is on her way."

Jesus. That was not going to be fun. She would be fussy and do everything in her power to make sure that she knew what was going on with him and Tamilya. She was worse that their coworkers at TFH.

She giggled; such a light-hearted sound filled his heart with joy.

"Oh, big, bad Marcus is afraid of his mama."

"Not afraid," he growled, which made her laugh even more.

"You are, but that's okay. She asked if the guest room was open."

Which meant she knew that Tamilya had been staying with him. Damn. Ashley Floyd could teach master spies a thing or two.

"Does that mean you're moving in with me?"

"Is that how you ask?" She shook her head.

He tightened his hold on her fingers. "Well?"

"I guess I could, but you know, I do like my house. It comes with a pool," she said with a teasing smile playing about her lips.

He let loose another growl and tugged her closer. She settled on the bed next to him, and they were still holding hands.

"Tell me," he said, and she knew what he meant without him saying it.

"The FBI is going to take over the case. We'll probably be called as witnesses if she doesn't plea."

He frowned. "I would like to see her rot, but I also want to get the bastards who were paying her."

She nodded. Then silence filled the room. Well, other than beeping sounds. They had time, and there was a bed…

He smiled.

"Absolutely not," she said.

He chuckled. "Come on, Tammy. You know you want to."

"Sometimes I would like to eat an entire cheesecake, but I don't because it's a bad idea."

He barked out a laugh and tugged her closer. She came willingly, easily. Without hesitation, she gave into his kiss, and he needed it. He needed that connection, that reality to know this was not a dream. He slid is tongue over the seam of her lips and she opened them. He stole inside trying his best to let her know that this was more than just right now. It was forever.

By the time she broke the kiss, pulling back slowly, they were both breathing heavily.

"Yep, you are that whole cheesecake."

The hum of arousal deepened her voice and he felt his cock responding.

"Tammy," he said warning her. She laughed.

"Sorry. You're just so easy."

"I am when it comes to you." She was smiling down at him, and he couldn't bear not to say it again. "I love you."

"I love you too, Marcus."

Before he could try to convince her into bed with him, the door opened and Del walked in.

"Hey, now, none of that," he said with a chuckle. Then he walked around the bed. "You look like shit."

"Well, I did get shot," Marcus said.

Del pulled out his phone texting someone.

"Are they still all here?" Tamilya asked.

Del nodded without looking up.

"Who?"

She smiled. "The TFH Ohana. They refused to leave."

As he heard the noise outside his door, he knew they were going to get reprimanded by the staff, but he didn't care. Everyone poured into the room. Someone flipped on the lights and Tamilya started to move away. He held on tight and she looked down at him with her eyebrows up.

"You stay right here."

For a long second, the noise of their coworkers filled the room and she said nothing. Then, a smile curved her mouth. She settled against him; their hands still entwined.

Marcus couldn't ask for anything more.

Epilogue

Three months later

Tamilya pressed her front against Marcus' back and slipped her arms around Marcus's waist as he pulled out the keycard to unlock their hotel room. His sister's wedding had gone off without a hitch, and Tamilya was feeling particularly frisky tonight.

She let her hands slide down, inching towards his crotch. He was so warm and sexy. And warm. She blinked even as she pawed at him. Maybe she'd had too much to drink because her mind wasn't really working right.

"Tammy," he said, but there was enough heat in his voice to diminish the warning she knew he was trying to give her.

"What?" she said, changing directions and easing her hands up to his chest.

He opened the door a second later and they tumbled into the room, almost falling onto the floor. Marcus saved both of them. He righted them, then turned to face her.

The passion in his gaze sent more heat spiraling through her, and a small dose of fear.

He stepped toward her and she squeaked and took off running. The fact that there was nowhere to run in their hotel room didn't compute in her champagne fueled head.

"Tammy," he said with a laugh as he caught hold of her. He swung her up into his arms and then laid her out on the bed. He covered her body with his. She felt his erection hard against her stomach. He smiled down at her, then it faded into a serious look.

Her heart quivered, as did her soul.

"What?" she asked fearing the worse. Was he going to screw this all up again? If he did, there was a good chance she would shoot him and dump his body in the Pacific.

"You know I love you, right?"

Her worries started to fade away as her heart filled with joy. "Yeah. Yeah, I do."

"Then be mine."

She blinked. "I am yours, Marcus."

"No," he said, reaching to open the bedside table drawer. He retrieved a little box. "I've been wanting to give this to you for weeks now, but, our families…"

He rolled his eyes. She knew exactly what he was saying without the words. Her parents and his mother had been completely in their business for the last couple of weeks. They hadn't had a night together since his mother and his sisters had hit the island eleven days, fifteen hours, and thirty minutes ago. Not that she was counting or anything.

He slipped off her and settled on the mattress beside her. He propped himself up on his elbow, then he opened the box and her heart almost stopped. Set against the white satin lining was an engagement ring. It was white gold, her preference, with one solitaire diamond. Emeralds dotted the band on either side of the diamond. Her eyes started to sting, and she realized she was about to cry. She hated to cry, even happy tears.

"I used my grandmother's diamond, then had it designed specifically for you." She kept staring at it and he sighed. "Say something, Tammy."

She looked up at him and her vision wavered. Dammit, she was going to cry. "It's so beautiful."

"Oh, baby, don't cry."

Tamilya sniffed and tried to control the tears, but she couldn't. She was so damned happy, and they just kept spilling over onto her cheeks.

"Say yes. Be mine."

She drew in a long breath, then looked into his eyes. "Only on two conditions," she said.

Suddenly, he looked apprehensive. "What?"

"First, you tell me exactly how you feel about me being in charge of our terrorism team." She had been bestowed the dubious honor the week before. It wasn't really a promotion in terms of money, but everyone would answer to her now when they had any terrorist threats.

"I have absolutely no problem."

The certainty in his voice warmed her heart. "Yeah?"

He nodded. "Del had told me he was thinking about moving you into the position, and I wholeheartedly agreed to it."

"You'll have to take orders from me."

"Tsk, I already take orders from you. But I have no problem following you at work. You're so fucking amazing at your job. I'm proud to work with you."

"Oh, damn," she said as a round of fresh tears filled

her eyes again. He set the ring on the bed between them and brushed away her tears.

"What was the second condition?"

She drew in her breath and released it slowly. "The only way I can be yours is if you will be mine also. Completely, on equal terms."

His face relaxed, the tension leaving his shoulders. "I can say yes, but the truth, we will never be on equal terms, Tammy. You're lightyears ahead of me and better than I deserve. But I want my ring on your finger and you in my bed, so I will agree to anything."

Joy filled her heart to bursting, and she felt her lips curl into a smile, then a grin. "Yes."

"Yes?" he asked, and she nodded.

He let out a whoop and took the ring out of the box, slipping it onto her finger.

"It fits."

"Of course it does," he said. "I had to get help from your mom to make sure."

A memory from a month ago hit her. Her mother had compared their fingers saying that they had the same sized hands. It was odd, but she'd been on her way to a meeting after they'd shared lunch and Tamilya had forgotten about it.

"So my parents know? You asked them?"

He frowned. "I did not ask, but I told them. You don't need your parents to speak for you. You're your own woman."

"Oh, Marcus," she said, her voice barely above a whisper. His love overwhelmed her at times, and she wasn't sure she would ever get used to it. He accepted her for who she was.

"So, soon-to-be Mrs. Lowe-Floyd—I'm assuming you

will at least hyphen our name—how about I show just how happy you made me?"

She leaned closer to accept a kiss, but he had other ideas. He shook his head and started slipping down her body, dragging the hem of her dress up and spreading her legs as he settled between them. He stilled and looked up at her.

"You were walking around at the wedding and reception with no panties on?" he asked, the sound of his voice rasping over her nerve endings. There was no doubt that it turned him on. Arousal shimmered in his voice. The sound of it fueled her own. "Thank God I didn't know about that, or we wouldn't have made it through the wedding."

She felt her face heat. She wasn't ashamed of her sexuality, but she had been so turned on sitting at the wedding without anything on under her dress. Seeing his reaction now added another layer of arousal to her already out of control libido.

"Such a wicked woman, and I am thankful for it. Now, let me show you how thankful."

His hot breath feathered against her sex right before she felt his mouth. His tongue slipped between her folds. She raised her knees, setting her feet on the mattress so she could press up. At the same time, Marcus slipped his hands beneath her rear end. Again and again, he pushed her near that edge, before yanking her back. She growled the last time he did it and he chuckled. The warm sound filled her soul, but it didn't help with her frustration.

"So impatient," he said mockingly, before taking her clit between his teeth.

Back and forth, he teased, then slipped two fingers into her. As she teetered on the edge, her entire body needing a release, he pulled away, but this time he grabbed a condom package, ripping it open and slipping it on. He took her by the hips and raised her up off the bed.

"Tamilya. Look at me."

She couldn't do anything less than that. In this one moment, she wanted to be connected on all levels. Body, mind, soul. He held her gaze as he thrust into her to the hilt. The motion slammed the headboard against the wall. He pulled out then pressed back in just as hard. Again and again, he thrust into her. Her sex clamped down hard on his cock, her orgasm slamming into her, washing over her. It was so fast and overwhelming that it stole her breath.

"Again," he said, not letting up on his rhythm. She came again, this time clamping down so hard on his shaft that he thrust only one more time before giving himself over to pleasure.

He collapsed on her and she wrapped her arms and legs around him. He was heavy, but she didn't care. Right now, this was the only place she wanted to be. He rolled them over to reverse their positions. He was still inside her. She felt his mouth brush against her temple.

Rising she smiled down at him. "I love you."

He returned her smile. "I love you too, Tammy."

She settled back down, tucking her head beneath his chin. Peace she hadn't felt in years filled her as she drifted off to sleep in his arms.

MAHALO FOR READING WICKED TEMPTATIONS. If you enjoyed Tamilya and Marcus' story, please consider leaving a review at your favorite online retailer or review site.

There are more TASK FORCE HAWAII to come in 2021, but make sure to check out some more of my romantic suspense books.

One-click—>SAVING THEA

She's determined to discover her mother's killer, and he is determined to protect the woman he loves.

From suspense and mystery, to hot sexy scenes, to tons of love. It is a hard book to put down.

Make sure to get SAVING THEA today!

LIKE WOLVES AND SUSPENSE? Check out—>PRIMAL INSTINCTS.

When a deranged killed targets Jacob's pack, he turns to the one woman who can help him save his friends and family, Sheriff Alexandra Littlefoot.

TFH TEAM BRAVO

Coming this October, a new chapter in the Task Force Hawaii Saga!

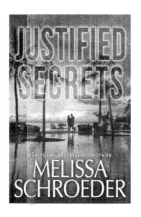

PREORDER TODAY

Everyone has secrets, but hers could get them both killed.

Autumn Bradford has always been a little...different. The

daughter of a cult leader, she has spent her life fighting the bad guys and searching for the father everyone thinks is dead. One thing stands in her way, the new leader of Team Bravo.

Former SEAL Seth Harrington accepted the job at TFH for a new start. Years of dangerous missions has left his body and soul scarred. He doesn't have time for a woman with too many secrets and the eating habits of a hobbit-no matter how attractive he finds her.

Autumn doesn't need a keeper or a protector, but every time she turns around, Seth seems to be there. Time together makes it difficult to avoid their attraction, and one stolen kiss makes it impossible to resist the temptation. Falling in love wasn't in the plans for either of them, but Seth realizes he will do anything to protect her, even if it means facing down the most dangerous man either of them know: her father.

Author Note: This is a Harmless World Novel with our favorite crime fighting heroes and heroines! There are secrets (duh!), inappropriate jokes, Hawaiian food, a betting pool as usual, a new team to get to know, and a training session that goes a little too far.

Meet the new team of Task Force Hawaii. Lead by former SEAL Seth Harrington, they focus on search and rescue, but also support Team Alpha.

Each member of TEAM Bravo will be pushed to the brink as they start their duty as the main search and rescue division of Task Force Hawaii.

TEAM MEMBERS

Captain: Seth Harrington
Ryan Morrison w/ rescue dog Maya
Nikki Kekoa
Robbie Ramirez
Kapone Hanson (Kap)

About the Author

From an early age, USA Today Best-selling author Melissa loved to read. When she discovered the romance genre, she started to listen to the voices in her head. After years of following her AF Major husband around, she is happy to be settled in Northern Virginia surrounded by horses, wineries, and many, many Wegmans.

Keep up with Mel, her releases, and her appearances by subscribing to her NEWSLETTER. If you want to keep up with cover reveals, new behind the scene info on her writing, and when new excerpts are posted, follow her MelissaSchroeder.net News News. Or you can do both! They are low traffic, so you will not get tons of emails.

Check out all her other books, family trees and other info at her website!
If you would want contact Mel, email her at: melissa@melissaschroeder.net

instagram.com/melschro

amazon.com/author/melissa_schroeder

facebook.com/MelissaSchroederfanpage

bookbub.com/authors/melissa-schroeder

goodreads.com/Melissa_Schroeder

tiktok.com/@melissawritesromance

Printed in Great Britain
by Amazon

46575685R00172